His gaze made her feel feminine.
Beautiful. Desirable.

A flush came over Angel's skin, a fine sheen that her grandmother used to refer to as a healthy glow. "Southern ladies never sweat, Angel," she would say. "We glow. Remember that. And always remember to be a lady."

Of course, being a lady was the furthest thing from Angel's mind right now. With Steve Thunderhorse—this impossibly sexy Sioux—looking at her with such raw hunger, what Angel had on her mind would make her grandmother cringe.

He was looking at her the way a man who wants to kiss a woman looks. Angel was certain of it. And she wanted him to kiss her. She wanted it more than anything she could remember wanting in her entire life.

D0804847

Dear Reader,

Happy anniversary! Twenty years ago, in May, 1980, we launched Silhouette Books. Much has changed since then, but our gratitude to you, our many readers, and our dedication to bringing you the best that romance fiction has to offer, remains as true today as it did in 1980. Thank you for sharing with us the joy of romance, and for looking toward a wonderful future with us. The best is yet to come!

Those winsome mavericks are back with brand-new stories to tell beneath the Big Sky! *The Kincaid Bride* by Jackie Merritt marks the launch of the MONTANA MAVERICKS: WED IN WHITEHORN series, which focuses on a new generation of Kincaids. This heartwarming marriage-of-convenience tale leads into Silhouette's exciting twelve-book continuity.

Romance is in the air in *The Millionaire She Married*, a continuation of the popular CONVENIENTLY YOURS miniseries by reader favorite Christine Rimmer. And searing passion unites a fierce Native American hero with his stunning soul mate in *Warrior's Embrace* by Peggy Webb.

If you enjoy romantic odysseys, journey to exotic El Bahar in *The Sheik's Arranged Marriage* by Susan Mallery—book two in the sizzling DESERT ROGUES miniseries.

Gail Link pulls heartstrings with her tender tale about a secret child who brings two lovebirds together in *Sullivan's Child*. And to cap off the month, you'll adore *Wild Mustang* by Jane Toombs—a riveting story about a raven-haired horse wrangler who sweeps a breathtaking beauty off her feet.

It's a spectacular month of reading in Special Edition. Enjoy!

All the best,

Karen Taylor Richman
Senior Editor

Please address questions and book requests to:
Silhouette Reader Service
U.S.: 3010 Walden Ave., P.O. Box 1325, Buffalo, NY 14269
Canadian: P.O. Box 609, Fort Erie, Ont. L2A 5X3

PEGGY WEBB
WARRIOR'S EMBRACE

Published by Silhouette Books

America's Publisher of Contemporary Romance

For Jane and Johnnie Sue, whose friendship undergirds me
with love, laughter, encouragement and a cockeyed can-do
optimism that keeps me going. Here's to the Big Three. Long
may we dance to the wild, unconventional rhythm of life.

And also to Jonathan White, my personal computer
wizard/angel, with heartfelt thanks.

 SILHOUETTE BOOKS

ISBN 0-373-24323-5

WARRIOR'S EMBRACE

Copyright © 2000 by Peggy Webb

Visit Silhouette at www.eHarlequin.com

Printed in U.S.A.

PEGGY WEBB

and her two chocolate Labs live in a hundred-year-old house not far from the farm where she grew up. "A farm is a wonderful place for dreaming," she says. "I used to sit in the hayloft and dream of being a writer." Now, with two grown children and more than forty-five romance novels to her credit, the former English teacher confesses she's still a hopeless romantic and loves to create the happy endings her readers love so well.

When she isn't writing, she can be found at her piano playing blues and jazz or in one of her gardens planting flowers. A believer in the idea that a person should never stand still, Peggy recently taught herself carpentry.

IT'S OUR 20th ANNIVERSARY!
We'll be celebrating all year,
Continuing with these fabulous titles,
On sale in May 2000.

Prologue

Saudi Arabia, February 1991

"Our greatest enemy is the one we can't see."

Steve stared at the line he'd typed. It was a good lead-in. Damned good. His editor would be pleased.

He slapped his cold hands together to get the circulation going, then continued writing his story. He had a deadline to meet, and the *Washington Post* didn't accept excuses.

Not that he'd ever made them. The more work he had, the better he liked it. "Keep this up," Mac had told him, "and you're a shoo-in for another Pulitzer."

Steve blew on the tips of his cold fingers and continued to type. Why should he complain? There were young men out there on the battlefront who were using socks for gloves.

"For the ground soldiers of Operation Desert Storm, the biggest fear is of chemical attack, a silent deadly enemy that strikes without warning. Gas masks and protective gear are heavy, but the soldiers carry them without complaint. They must, for otherwise, they risk a slow and torturous death from an enemy they cannot even see."

The steady movement of the cursor and the rapid rat-a-tat of the keys fueled Steve's ardor. He loved his work—loved the travel, loved the excitement, even loved the risks. Emily would divorce him if she knew of the close calls he'd had trying to get exactly the right photo to go with his stories.

Steve stopped typing long enough to blow a kiss to the photo on the edge of his makeshift desk—his wife and four-year-old daughter emerging from the swimming pool, laughing. He'd snapped them last summer.

"Don't think of summer," he told himself. Even in two pairs of wool socks, his toes were turning to icicles.

Steve continued typing. "Life at the front—"

Sergeant Barry Wilkes interrupted him in midsentence.

"Hey, Thunderhorse. You've got a call from home. They said it was urgent."

Flat tires were urgent to Emily. She was probably wondering which garage to call.

Steve picked up the phone. "Thunderhorse here," he said.

Through the static he heard the news from home. And when it was finished, he would gladly have walked into the battle without chemical gear. He would gladly have taken a bullet. He would gladly have breathed the lethal gas.

With tears freezing on his face, he finally understood the truth: The greatest agony was not dying; it was living.

Chapter One

Mississippi, 2000

It was one of those golden autumn days that made Angel Mercer want to be outside running barefoot through the leaves. That was one thing she loved about Mississippi; even in fall she could go barefoot if she wanted to. She could plant her feet solidly on the earth; she could press her toes down in it and feel its power and its promise.

Her toes started itching, so she kicked off her shoes and was halfway out of her chair when the blinking green cursor called her back. If she gave in to every wild urge she had, she'd never get her new book off the ground.

"Chapter One," she typed, and then sat staring at the screen as if she'd never heard of her major character, let alone made her a household word.

Angel sighed. Sometimes she wished she was still writing cozy little mysteries about Susan and her cat named Fox who did nothing more than come across an occasional stolen rare book from the stacks of Mulberry Library. Her sales had been decent, her income modest and the expectations average. Angel could walk out her door any given Tuesday and go to the supermarket to buy tomatoes without a soul stopping to ask for her autograph. She could eat peanut butter and crackers on her front porch without anybody stopping to gawk.

Nobody except Mabel down at the *Oxford Crier* wanted interviews, and nobody drove all the way from Minnesota to camp outside her door, looking for a miracle.

But, that was before she'd created Muriel, the sassiest angel this side of heaven whose love for miracles was exceeded only by her love for gumshoeing.

"An overnight sensation," the press had written about Angel after the first Muriel book came out. Reporters didn't seem to care that she'd slogged away at her craft for five years and that she'd already solved eight crimes. In her books, of course. Susan and Fox enjoyed a brief resurrection on the coattails of Muriel, then they faded into out-of-print oblivion.

Just on general principles, Angel erased "Chapter One" and typed it all over again. Getting a fresh start. Hoping her muse would be with her.

"Angel." Her dad peered around the door frame. "I don't mean to interrupt, honey."

"You're not an interruption, Dad, you're a welcome distraction." She shoved back from her desk. "Come on in."

"I was just thinking about the benefit."

Standing in the doorway, her dad looked distinguished and fit, a silver-haired retired history professor who never went to the square in Oxford without being stopped by half-a-dozen former students. It was only when he walked that his ill health showed. A light stroke, brought on by years of diabetes, had left him with a limp. He eased into the chair across from her desk, then smiled at her.

"You look mighty pretty today, sweetheart."

"And you look mighty handsome." Angel left her chair to stand beside him and ruffle his hair. "What about the benefit, Dad?"

"You know Kaki. She's wanting to put on the dog again, everybody gussied up in tuxedos and wishing they were home watching reruns of *Mash*."

Angel laughed. She knew without consulting her research assistant/secretary that her dad had perfectly described what Kaki wanted for the annual diabetes benefit. She was the formal type. Even though Angel had told her it was all right to come to work in shorts and jeans and barefoot, too, if she wanted, she always arrived promptly at eight dressed in a suit with matching pumps and purse, her hair done up in a French twist, looking closer to sixty than the fifty Angel knew her to be. Carl Mercer's opinion of Kaki, which he privately expressed to his daughter, was that she needed somebody besides him to tell her that she was beautiful. To back up what he said, he'd made it one of his life's missions to find Kaki a man. On the sly, of course. He would never let on to Kaki.

"I wish you'd just speak to her," Carl added. "She won't listen to a goldarn thing I say."

"I'll do better than that. I'll tell her that since you're the guest of honor, we're going to let you plan the shindig this year. You can have whatever you want. A three-ring circus, if you like."

Carl was so pleased Angel wondered why she hadn't thought of the idea years ago. He was a brilliant man without nearly enough to keep him busy. Maybe if he had the benefit on his mind, he'd ease up on going to the cemetery so often. Angel had loved her mother, too, but all those conversations of his with the dead seemed excessive.

"Maybe that's what I'll have." Carl patted her hand. "I've made some tea. You want a glass?"

"With pear juice and lemon?"

"Just the way you like it. We can sit on the front porch. A breeze has sprung up, and I spotted a pair of blue birds in the pecan tree."

Angel kicked off her shoes and took her tea to the front-porch swing and sat with her dad, swaying gently, not saying anything, just letting the peace seep into their souls. Blessedly, the sidewalk was empty of fans.

"I could sit here for hours," she said.

"I hate to be the one to burst that bubble." Kaki's voice came through the screen door, then she appeared, spectator pumps, pink linen suit and all. "Jenny's on the phone."

Angel stood up. "Here. You can have my seat. But I'll be wanting it back."

"Pink becomes you, Kaki," she heard her dad say as she went inside. "You should wear it more often."

Angel smiled. What the world needed were more Carl Mercers.

"Hello," she said into the phone, then smiled as her agent began reading reviews from Angel's latest book, *Angel in Camelot.* As usual, Jenny Cordova had censored the reviews, reading only the glowing ones.

"What did Lucy have to say?"

"Lucretia Borgia? That witch." Jenny's words conveyed exactly what she thought of L.A.'s premier book reviewer. Over the years she'd called Angel everything from a hack writer without an original thought in her head to a Mary Higgins Clark wannabe. Never mind that the books she panned all made the number-one slot on the *New York Times* list.

"I guess I can live without another wound."

"Are you wounded, Angel? Tell Mother Jenny all about it."

Angel hooted. "Mother Jenny, my fanny."

Jenny Cordova was the least-motherly person she'd ever met. With her penchant for wild earrings and wild clothes, not to mention her untamed mane of flaming-red hair, she was the epitome of bohemian. On the other hand, she was the best listener, as well as the best friend, Angel had ever had.

"I'm having trouble starting my new book."

"Good Lord, you don't have to pitch right in and start writing. Why don't you give your mind a rest? Take a vacation. Go somewhere with a fabulous man."

"Britt offered to take me to the Bahamas." Britt Ace, the world's sexiest TV anchor, according to the polls, and Angel's ex-fiancé.

"I said *fabulous,* darling."

Jenny made no secret of her dislike for Britt. She considered him pompous and false, and she'd said so to his face. By the same token, he always asked her where she'd parked her broom. Sometimes Angel laughed at the barbs they sent flying at each other, but mostly she wondered what her life would be like if she had actually said yes to a man who couldn't get along with her best friend.

"Now, Jenny, he might have been a tad overbearing as a fiancé, but as a friend he's hard to beat." Angel's reproof was only halfhearted. Lately with Britt she'd felt like one of those exotic birds she'd seen in cages at the zoo.

"A tad? He makes Hitler look like Mickey Mouse. Has he pressed you for another of those hideous up-close-and-personal features?"

"Not lately."

"Thank God for small favors." Mercifully Jenny dropped

the subject. "But that's not why I called, sweetie. I've got three studios looking to do a film deal on *Angel in Camelot* and all three major networks squawking for an interview. Of course, you-know-who thinks he has an edge."

Just then Carl burst through the front door with Kaki right behind him, tight-lipped.

"A carload of Texans just pulled up and are now tromping through your petunias taking souvenir pictures," Kaki said as she herded Carl into the kitchen. "You can't even drink your tea in peace around here."

"Good grief." Angel sank onto the floor where she sat with her knees to her chest and the receiver clutched to her ear.

"Angel…Angel, what's wrong, sweetie?"

"I think I'm going crazy, Jenny."

There was a long silence at Jenny's end of the line, followed by her voice, full of love and concern. "It's time to take that vacation, honey. Go someplace where nobody will know who you are."

"Actually I've been thinking about getting a camper and going out West."

"For God's sake. With rattlesnakes and sidewinders?"

"I think they're the same thing, Jenny. Anyhow, you said go where nobody will know me."

"Yeah, but I meant somewhere with room service and waiters tripping all over themselves to do your every bidding."

"I need to do this, Jenny. By myself."

The long silence at the other end of the line was eloquent. Jenny was probably thinking what Britt would have said, and had said on many occasions: "Angel you need somebody to take care of you." She guessed she would still be with him if he hadn't tried so hard to control her.

Even Kaki thought Angel needed a keeper, though she was much more subtle in expressing her feelings.

That was the way of people. Make one mistake and they never let you forget it.

Of course, neither could Angel. She'd been twenty-two, fresh out of college, looking for a job, excited about her future. And along came Dan Calloway, every girl's dream, every girl's nightmare. Handsome, charming and glib, he'd promised her everlasting love on a ranch in Texas. What she'd gotten was a two-room shanty fifty miles from civilization with a man whose idea of being a husband was to keep her a virtual prisoner. "A prisoner of love," he would croon, caressing her hair, all the while denying her the use of the car, the telephone and even the bathroom when he got in one of his moods.

It was six months of sheer hell.

She'd finally managed one desperate call to her father from a gas station on Interstate 10. He'd come to get her with two private investigators backing him up.

But in spite of the mess he'd had to clean up, her father was still the only person in Angel's life who trusted her to take care of herself.

Sometimes when the blues got her down, he would say, "You're a champ, sweetheart, and don't you ever forget it."

And so now she said to Jenny, "I'm a champ, Jenny, and don't you ever forget it."

Carl went with his daughter to buy a camper, secondhand so nobody would suspect it was her, Angel had said. Later, sitting cross-legged on the floor with maps spread all around her, Angel decided she'd head west.

"Toward Arizona." It would take her beyond Texas, and she needed to get beyond Texas. Besides, she'd always been fascinated with the West, particularly the history of the Old West.

Her interest was due in part to her father, who was sitting in his favorite chair, a copy of Dee Brown's *Bury My Heart at Wounded Knee* open on his lap.

"Come with me, Dad."

He shook his head. "Not this time, honey. What would Frances think if I went off and left her this time of year?"

"Dad," Angel chided gently.

Not that she was worried. Carl Mercer was far too sensible and intelligent to go off the deep end, but she hated to see her father still so wrapped up in her mother three years after her death. They'd been married in the fall, and he always carried flowers to her grave on their anniversary.

"I'm all right, honey. Don't you worry about me."

"I'm not worried, Dad. I just thought it would be fun for the two of us to tool around the West together. We could even buy ten-gallon hats and act like real dudes."

The hall clock struck ten, and Carl stood up, yawning.

"Bedtime for old people." He kissed his daughter on the top of her head. "You'll have fun, honey, and don't you forget to keep your maps handy and look at your compass. I don't want my daughter lost in the wild and woolly West."

"Not a chance, Dad. Besides, I can always stop and ask directions."

Which proved to be easier said than done.

Angel climbed down from her camper beside the lone gas pump and sauntered toward the weathered-plank building with the oversize sign on front that said Welcome to Broken Arrow. Two middle-aged men leaned on the counter eating candy bars and talking to an older man behind the cash register. Conversation ceased when she walked in.

She waited for the outcries of recognition, but none came. She felt greatly encouraged, even triumphant.

"Which way to Arizona?" she asked.

The three men laughed till tears rolled down their cheeks. Angel didn't think her question was all that funny. Besides, she didn't care to be laughed at by strangers. Furthermore, she was tired and hungry and feeling mean.

Five days of driving does that to a woman.

"That joke was free," she snapped. "The next time I'm charging admission."

She wheeled around with the full intention of stalking out of that town no bigger than a flea and trying to decipher her map, but a hand on her shoulder stopped her.

"Hold on there, miss. We're not poking fun at you. Your question just struck us as funny, that's all."

The man was sincere and his voice was kind, and Angel really didn't want to stalk off at all. What she wanted was an extra large chocolate bar with almonds. And maybe a side order of steak. If she knew where to find it.

Somebody who couldn't find something as big as Arizona was bound to have a hard time finding something as small as a steak.

"I didn't mean to act uppity. I'm just tired and hungry."

"You come a long way, miss?" This from the man behind the counter. On second glance he looked very much like her father.

"All the way from Oxford, Mississippi."

"Headed to Arizona, are you?"

"Well, I thought so. If I can ever find it."

He let out a full-bellied chuckle. "You're in Arizona."

She laughed with him. In relief, mostly. She was tired of driving, and now she could stop. She'd arrived at her destination.

Wouldn't Britt be surprised—when she decided to talk to

him. Before she'd left home he'd had the audacity to suggest she ditch the camper and fly out, or at the very least, hire a driver.

"I can't imagine you on the road by yourself, Angel. You'll get lost, and right now I'm too busy to come and rescue you."

He didn't give her credit for anything. Except being a good writer.

"I have the instincts of a homing pigeon," she'd told him. "For your information I don't need rescuing."

But of course, that was the first thing she'd needed. Here she was in Arizona and didn't even know it. She wasn't about to tell Britt or Jenny or Kaki.

Nor was she going to tell them that she hadn't had the heart to drive through Texas. She'd detoured all the way up through Arkansas and Oklahoma to avoid the place she was trying so hard to forget.

"Well, then, that settles it. I guess I can stop driving now. I think I'll have an extra large Hershey bar with almonds."

She'd always had a knack for conversing with strangers, and she settled comfortably beside them while she ate her candy. Before Muriel had taken off as if she had wings, Angel used to travel around with her books, signing a copy at the drop of a hat for anybody who did her the least kindness—a waitress who told her the apple pie was better than the lemon, a taxi driver who recommended a good show to see, even an old lady with a dog that didn't mind being petted.

Nowawdays, pulling out one of her books would bring on a media circus. She missed the old days of anonymity.

"Can you recommend a good motel?" she asked her newfound friends—Ben at the cash register, Luke eating chocolate and Jim eating butter-crunch.

The bathroom in her camper was the size of a telephone booth, and she longed for a good soak in a big tub.

"The nearest one is about a hundred miles," Ben told her. She made no move to hide her distress. "You might want to try that campground up the road a piece."

She wished she'd asked Ben to be more specific about where "up the road a piece" was. Or better still, asked him to draw a map.

"Muriel, why can't I conjure up miracles as easily in real life as I do in books?" she said.

And suddenly there was the sign. Broken Arrow Campground, left, three miles. And right underneath it a sign that proclaimed WILD WEST SHOW, starring THUNDER-HORSE, left, one mile.

Angel whooped for joy. She was in the West, wasn't she? She might as well put on that ten-gallon hat she'd bought in Arkansas and see if she couldn't learn to ride a thunderhorse, whatever that was.

Chapter Two

The crowd was small today. Mostly children with a token adult or two. The man peering through the curtains was pleased. The thing he loved most about doing his shows was the chance it gave him to bring bits of Native American history alive in such a way that the teaching was subtle and the learning painless.

Today he decided he would start out with his Sitting Bull routine. It was a great attention getter, and he knew if he captured the imaginations of the children in the first act, he'd have them for the rest of the show.

He lowered the edge of the curtain and turned back to his dressing room, a makeshift area behind the arena. A breeze stirred the canvas sides of his tent as he donned his costume, reminding him how quickly the seasons were passing.

Over the last nine years, time had blurred for him, and that was a good thing. He'd carved out a simple life for himself, one full of the pleasures of nature—the sun on his face, the earth under his feet and the wind at his back. His possessions were few, his freedom unlimited. He traveled when the need for companionship, however brief, overtook him, and he retreated to his ranch near Sedona when he craved solitude.

There was a brief stir beyond the curtain as latecomers found seats for the show. He lifted his face toward the sky and petitioned the Great Spirit to help him do honor to his mighty Sioux ancestor. Then, dressed in beaded leggings and carrying a single-shot muzzle loader, a bow and quiver, and a thunderbird shield, he walked into the arena as Sitting Bull.

"Good afternoon. I am Thunderhorse."

You could have knocked her down with a feather, Angel thought. That was how light-headed she felt. Not only was the man in the arena the most delicious-looking thing she'd ever laid eyes on, but she remembered—quite vividly—what she'd thought when she first read the sign.

Obviously this was a horse of a different breed. Sioux, as a matter of fact. At least that was what he was telling his audience, and she had no reason to believe it was not true. He had the high cheekbones, the long black hair, the bronze skin. Native American was stamped all over him.

Full blood, that was what he was saying now.

He had gorgeous legs. Thick columns of muscle beautifully displayed in the buckskin leggings.

What was he saying about Sitting Bull?

Angel dragged her wandering mind away from his glorious body and tried to concentrate on the show.

"Sitting Bull was the last of the great Sioux chiefs to surrender to the U.S. government when they began herding Native Americans onto reservations. He fled to Canada with his loyal following for a few years, and when he finally returned to the U.S., he had become a folk hero.''

The children around her were enraptured—and so was Angel. The man was mesmerizing. It wasn't merely his voice, though certainly that was memorable—deep, rich and sonorous. It wasn't merely the costume, though she'd never seen better. Authentic, if she guessed right. And it wasn't merely his presence, though that certainly was commanding.

There was something mystical about Thunderhorse, as if he had somehow tapped into an unknown source that fed assurance and magnetism straight into his bloodstream.

He stood quietly while he talked, and yet he gave the impression of power in motion.

''In 1883, when the Northern Pacific Railroad drove the last spike into its transcontinental track, officials invited the great Sioux chief to give the welcoming speech at opening ceremonies.

''Of course, very few people spoke Sioux, so Sitting Bull was assigned a young army officer who worked with him on the speech and who would later interpret it to the audience.

''How many of you have read in your history books that Sitting Bull gave the speech?''

Hands went up all over the audience. Some of them yelled, ''Me! I have!'' Caught up in their enthusiasm, Angel stuck her hand up, too.

''Did your history books tell you what Sitting Bull said?''

A chorus of no's echoed through the crowd, while Thunderhorse stood on stage, smiling. Smiling and waiting.

''I'm going to deliver the speech for you today, just as Sitting Bull did back in 1883 in Bismarck, North Dakota.''

Thunderhorse moved to the center of the arena, and when the spotlight flooded him, the audience gasped. Not only

had he added an old army hat, he'd somehow *become* Sitting
Bull. Then with solemn dignity, he began to speak.

"You have taken away our land and made us outcasts,"
he said.

A hush fell over the audience. This was a history lesson
the children would never forget.

Nor would Angel, for she was listening with her heart.

"Is it wrong for me to love my own? Is it wicked for me
because my skin is red? Because I am a Sioux? Because I
was born where my father lived? Because I would die for
my people and my country?"

Thunderhorse paused, and the children broke into wild
applause. Then, nodding his head and bowing slightly, he
continued his speech.

"If the Great Spirit had desired me to be a white man,
he would have made me so in the first place. He put in your
heart certain wishes and plans. In my heart he put other and
different desires."

Wild applause. Dignified acknowledgment.

"Each man is good in the sight of the Great Spirit."
Every word was a thunderbolt, sent directly into the heart
of his audience.

"It is not necessary for eagles to be crows. Now we are
poor, but we are free. No white man controls our footsteps.
If we must die, we die defending our rights."

Thunderhorse waved and bowed and smiled, and the children cheered.

"What do you think happened after Sitting Bull gave that
speech?" he asked his young listeners.

"Nobody understood him," a little blond girl called.

"Come over here." The girl left her second-row seat, and
Thunderhorse placed a beaded necklace in her hand. "Tell
us your name and where you're from."

"I'm Carolyn Withers and I'm from Texas!"

All her friends cheered.

Angel grinned. Little Miss Carolyn Withers was either a cheerleader or getting an early start on being Miss America.

"Miss Carolyn Withers from Texas, you are exactly right. The only person who understood Sitting Bull was the interpreter. The audience clapped and cheered while Sitting Bull smiled and insulted them. Afterward, the interpreter stood up and gave such a flowery interpretation of the speech that Sitting Bull was invited by the railroad officials to speak at St. Paul."

The spotlight followed them as Thunderhorse escorted the little girl back to her seat, stopping to chat with the children who reached out to touch his costume. While he was busy distracting his audience, a shadow emerged from behind the curtains and walked quietly into the center of the arena.

The sound of drums filled the tent, and the spotlight swung to the center of the arena. A white stallion tossed his head and pawed the ground, and the children clapped until their hands were red.

Accompanied by drumbeats, Thunderhorse told how Sitting Bull had joined Buffalo Bill Cody's Wild West Show and had traveled throughout Europe wearing a white sombrero and riding his white horse.

Thunderhorse fired his gun, and the stallion sat on his haunches and raised one hoof in the air. Thunderhorse fired a second time, and the stallion began to gallop around the ring. The rhythm of drumbeats increased, then Thunderhorse tensed and sprang onto the back of the stallion.

The animal reared into the air while the drumbeats faded, then gave way to the "Blue Danube Waltz." Horse and rider became one graceful creature, moving in three-quarter time.

Then the white stallion left the ring, still prancing to the rhythm of the music. Suddenly the massive glorious animal was standing in front of Angel's chair, his rider smiling down at her.

"May I have this dance?" Thunderhorse said.

"Oh, yes!"

Eager as a child, Angel jumped out of her chair. But there was nothing at all childlike about her feelings as Thunderhorse bent down and swept her onto the stallion. Quite simply, she thought she had died and gone to heaven.

The woman in his arms was soft and sweet-smelling, and even prettier up close.

Angel Mercer. He'd recognized her immediately. You couldn't walk into a bookstore without seeing her photograph on the cover of dust jackets. It had struck him as odd that she would be sitting in his big top in the middle of Arizona without an escort, without another person to protect her. And she needed protecting. In spades.

Her vulnerability showed a mile away. That was the second thing he'd noticed about her. After the blue eyes.

Angel Mercer had the most incredible blue eyes he'd ever seen. Like pieces of sky. Like violets after the rain.

Steve Thunderhorse hadn't written poetry in years. Hadn't written *anything* in years. Hadn't wanted to. Not even when he picked up the newspaper and scanned the columns by war correspondents.

Let somebody else cover the wars. Let somebody else make the sacrifices. Let somebody else pay the awful price.

Quickly he reined in his runaway thoughts. His act didn't take much concentration. He and the stallion had performed it hundreds of times. The horse needed no direction from him.

Thank the Great Spirit.

What had possessed him to pick the one person in the audience who could get under his skin? Why hadn't he picked that little old lady on the front row? The one with the big red purse and the tightly permed yellow hair. She looked like somebody with a strapping husband and six kids waiting for her at home, somebody who would face down a grizzly bear if the occasion called for it, somebody who would laugh as she climbed aboard his dancing horse, then laugh when he put her back in her seat and forgot about her.

"Oh, my. Isn't this wonderful?" Angel sighed, then settled back against him.

Actually, melted would be a better term. Leaning against him, she felt boneless. And fragile.

His nobility was showing again. Thunderhorse brought it under tight control. He hadn't been a hero to anybody in nine years—and didn't intend to be one now. Heroes didn't let the people they loved die.

Angel half turned, and her soft hair brushed his cheek. "Imagine, a dancing horse... I could dance like this forever."

So could Thunderhorse. And there was the rub.

His arms trembled with the effort not to tighten around this soft appealing woman as "Blue Danube" played on.

He thought the music would never end.

Angel didn't want the music to end. She could taste her disappointment when the last strain died away.

Thunderhorse didn't speak as he guided the stallion back to her chair, didn't say a thing as he dismounted and helped her down.

Had she done something wrong? Was she supposed to bow or wave or pet the horse? Or pet the owner?

Now there was an idea worthy of pursuit. She could think of a dozen ways she'd like to pet Thunderhorse, and that was just for starters. He was bending over her, looking deeply into her eyes, and her creative mind was off and running.

Wasn't this the part where the boy was supposed to kiss the girl? Wasn't that what Roy Rogers and Dale Evans always did at the end of a performance?

Waves of applause washed over them while she stood helpless under his intense gaze. *Oh, help.* Where were words when she needed them?

Something flickered in the depths of his black eyes and he turned to go. Then...then the world stood still.

He turned back to her—a fraction of a second, so quickly nobody noticed, so swiftly she might have dreamed it—and brushed his finger lightly across her lips.

She parted them in pure astonishment, in pure delight. For an insane moment she expected to see rockets bursting in the air, lightning streaking across the sky. All this inside a rather shabby tent in the middle of the Wild West.

Then abruptly, he was gone, back in the center ring doing bareback tricks on his white horse. Electrified, alive in a way she hadn't been for years, Angel sat in her chair and wondered if there was a second show.

And whether he would notice if she stayed.

Chapter Three

The campground was deep in a canyon surrounded by cottonwood trees and red rocks stacked straight to the sky. A setting sun painted brilliant colors across the high-desert country and created purple shadows a man could contemplate forever. Peace was in every ripple of the branches overhead, in the call of the lone eagle soaring toward the peaks, in the whisper of underbrush stirred by the activities of desert creatures.

Thunderhorse leaned back in his chair, sipped his evening cup of coffee and let the tranquillity soak into his soul.

He had a roof over his head, food in his belly and freedom. What more did a man need? What more could he want?

With summer vacation over and kids headed back to school, the campground was empty this time of year except for his camper and the one on the far side of the campground belonging to the caretaker.

Thunderhorse considered himself lucky. As much as he enjoyed his audiences, especially the children, he was even fonder of solitude. It was getting time to pack up the show and go back to his ranch and claim that blessed aloneness.

Besides, Lucas Gray Wolf would be getting antsy. He got that way every year during the Moon of the Falling Leaves. Let the first leaf turn red, and Lucas was off on his bike, swapping his Stetson for a helmet that would protect his hard head on another of his many mysterious adventures.

The least Thunderhorse could do was go home and let his partner have his freedom. He owed Lucas that—and so much more.

If it hadn't been for his best friend, in fact, Thunderhorse would still be in a rehab clinic somewhere in D.C.—or dead in the gutter.

Suddenly the eagle stopped his lazy soaring and sailed straight out of sight, and the rustling in the underbrush ceased. Someone was coming.

No sooner had Thunderhorse thought this, when he heard the chug of an engine and a camper moved into view. Disappointment slashed him. He'd begun to feel almost as if he owned the whole canyon.

Fortunately there was plenty of room in the campground. The camper pulling in didn't necessarily mean he had to talk to anybody.

At the entrance the driver paused, talking to the caretaker, then headed straight for the slot next to Thunderhorse.

He watched a moment, disbelieving, then left his chair and went into his trailer. There went his solitude.

He could move of course, but that would mean changing hookups. And he was leaving in a few days, anyway. Surely he could endure next-door neighbors that long. Maybe he'd get lucky and they'd be the quiet types. Or the type who left early in the morning to go sight-seeing and didn't return till bedtime.

If he played his cards right, he might never even see them.

Out his window he glimpsed the trailer backing into the slot next to his. The neighborly thing would be to go outside and help the man with his hookup.

Let the caretaker do that. Thunderhorse wasn't feeling neighborly.

Instead, he picked up a book and settled into a chair for a quiet read. A loud thump followed by the grinding of metal against metal shattered his solitude.

"What the devil...?"

His whole camper shook as metal scraped against metal once more. Thunderhorse leaped out of his chair and stalked to his door.

He'd hauled his camper nearly a hundred thousand miles with nary a mishap, and here he was sitting in his own living room reading a book while some idiot backed into him.

There would be hell to pay.

Thunderhorse looked at the trailer rammed into his, a secondhand job that had seen better days. Wasn't that always the way? He'd bet they didn't have a penny's worth of insurance.

He glanced at the driver's seat, planning to skewer the accident-prone jerk with a fierce scowl, but the driver had already left and was headed around the camper.

"Oh, dear!" she said. "It's you."

Angel Mercer stood two feet away, her big blue eyes awash with tears, and Thunderhorse couldn't have held on to his scowl if his life had depended on it.

Why me? he wondered. He'd encountered this angel twice in one day. Were the fates conspiring against him?

"I'm so terribly sorry," she said. "I guess I'm not a very good driver."

"Nonsense. Anybody can make a mistake."

Was that him talking? He couldn't believe it. Not only was he soothing her, he was planning to help her—with anything she needed.

He had to be out of his mind.

"Why don't you sit over there in my lawn chair and let me see what I can do about this?" he said.

On the bright side, at least she'd have insurance. Which was the least of his worries at the moment. The problem was nobody had insured him against blond blue-eyed angels who showed up on his doorstep in tears.

Angel couldn't seem to stop crying. It wasn't that she minded paying for the damage. That was nothing to her. Shoot, she could buy him a new camper. It wasn't even that she minded being thought of as somebody who couldn't drive worth a darn.

No, the thing that made her unable to stop crying was that Thunderhorse was the one she'd run into. *Thunderhorse,* of all people. The man who had already made her forget everything about her life, including her quest for independence. Even worse, he was turning out to be a genuine hero, somebody who took one look at her and knew everything she needed, including kindness.

She wiped her wet face with her hand, then leaned back in the lawn chair and closed her eyes. After five days on the road all by herself, it was a pure relief to sit and have somebody else take care of her. She was so tired she didn't know what to do.

Tomorrow she'd go back to taking care of herself. Tomorrow she'd quit needing to be rescued.

He was back there somewhere, hidden between trailers, and when he reappeared, she jumped.

"It's not so bad," he said. "Nothing some paint and a good whack with a rubber mallet won't fix."

"I'm so glad. Of course, I'll pay for everything. It was all my fault."

"I just happened to be in your way, that's all."

Though he deadpanned the words, his eyes were crinkled with laughter. Angel chuckled. She did like a man with a sense of humor.

"I never introduced myself. I'm Angel Mercer."

"I know who you are."

"Oh?"

"I read."

He vanished between the trailers again, and she was left to wonder what he'd meant. Did that mean he'd read her books? Did it mean he liked them? He didn't like them?

Angel sighed. It was just like her to go searching for ulterior motives and hidden meanings in every word.

She was on vacation, for goodness' sake. Couldn't she just let things be? Couldn't she just let herself get carried along by events without wondering about the consequences, about how it would all end?

This was her life, not some plot she'd hatched for one of her novels. She took a deep breath, squared her shoulders, then got up from her chair.

"Need any help back there?"

"No."

The man didn't talk much. That could be a good thing or it could be a bad thing. Did it mean he wasn't interested in talking to her? Or did it mean he was merely the quiet type?

The way he'd ridden that white stallion he didn't appear to be the quiet type. More the daring buccaneer, the noble savage, the fierce warrior, the—

"You could stand over there by the cat's claw and direct while I drive yours out," he said.

"All right." She started off, then abruptly turned back. "What's the cat's claw?"

"Sorry, I forgot." He pointed in the direction of a bush that had lethal-looking burrs. "Over there."

She stood beside the bush, but not too close. Forgot what? That she wasn't Native American?

That she wasn't from Arizona? That she was a woman?

"Ready?" he called.

"I'm always ready," she said.

This time he didn't try to disguise his grin.

"Ready for every emergency," she amended.

"Certainly," he said, then disappeared into her camper.

She wished she could have seen his face.

Did that mean he was agreeing with her? Having a little joke at her expense?

Thunderhorse stuck his head out the window. "How am I doing?" he yelled.

"Great! Just great!"

Doing about what? Disengaging their trailers? Driving in a straight line?

Stealing her heart?

Good grief, where had that come from? She was definitely suffering road fatigue. As soon as he got her trailer parked in the slot, she was going straight to bed and sleeping for twelve hours.

"There, that ought to do it," he said.

"Thanks."

Thunderhorse was standing beside her, so close she could see how the sun burnished his cheekbones. They seemed a mile high.

"You look as if you could use a little nourishment," he said. "I was thinking about going down the road to a place that serves the best steak this side of the Mississippi. Care to join me?''

''Of course I do.''

Her stomach shouted with joy.

And so did the rest of her.

Chapter Four

It was that beautiful time of evening when the sky still glowed faintly with residual rays from a vanished sun. Colors softened. Breezes lifted. Stillness descended on the land.

As far as Thunderhorse was concerned, it was the perfect time of day. And he was traveling with the perfect woman to enjoy it. She didn't try to fill the silence with useless chatter. She didn't fidget and swivel her head like a tourist and call out exclamations about this or that.

She merely relaxed and, if the soft smile playing around her lips was any indication, enjoyed.

A man could get used to having a woman like that around.

Angel leaned her head against the backrest and closed her eyes. Blond hair spilled across dark leather. The stuff of poetry and dreams.

Thunderhorse forced his gaze back to the road.

"I could ride like this forever," she said.

"That's what you said this afternoon about dancing."

She opened her eyes and smiled at him. "You remember?"

"Yes."

He remembered every tiny detail—the way her hair felt against his cheek; the way her hips fit into his, as if they were made for exactly that purpose; the way she smelled, like honeysuckle in the early-morning dew; the way her eyes turned darker when she was happy.

He remembered too much, too much for a man bent on spending the rest of his life without attachments.

"Are we going far?" she asked. Then, "I hope so."

He smiled. How had somebody as artless as Angel managed to avoid being chewed to pieces by the media?

"We'll go as far as you want to go. We can drive around until you get hungry."

"I'm starving, but I'd rather look than eat. This country fills the soul."

"Yes, it does."

Somehow he counted it as a personal victory that Angel had so quickly recognized the heart of his homeland.

"I can act as tour guide and point things out to you, or you can just look. Whichever you prefer."

"I want to just soak it all in, willy-nilly."

He smiled. He'd guessed she might say that. Writers gleaned facts from pouring through books and interviewing people, but their inspiration came from *absorbing,* undisturbed.

Once, eons ago…

Pushing the thought from his mind, Thunderhorse turned down a winding canyon road. He watched Angel out of the corner of his eye, appreciating the play of fading light and shadow across her face, the occasional smile as something she'd seen caught her fancy, the way she could stay focused on a distant rock without moving a muscle.

As they rounded a curve, they came upon the Verde River, lush with willows along its banks, a wide swath of autumn gold in the midst of a land painted with bold reds and oranges.

"Oh, would you stop right here?" she asked.

"Yes."

He didn't ask why. Something was calling to her soul, probably the same thing he felt every time he saw the river rushing through the high desert: the age-old pull of nature at its finest, the certainty that as long as there was this beauty, this design, this order, the earth would surely endure.

Thunderhorse crossed the bridge and parked beside a cottonwood tree. A fisherman hoping for a late catch before dark caught sight of her and waved. She waved back, then called down to him, "Catch anything?" as if he might be her next-door neighbor or somebody she'd known since first grade.

He pulled his stringer out of the water and held it up for her to see.

"Bravo." She smiled at him, then moved on down the river past a couple of Japanese tourists, careful not to walk in front of the camera they had trained on the scene.

Feeling by turns strangely content and unusually restless, Thunderhorse walked beside her. In case she tripped on a rock, he told himself. Or came upon a sidewinder. Or took a misstep and tumbled down the embankment toward the river.

Protecting her. Watching over her.

Something cold twisted in his gut, and he sat down on a large rock while she meandered away. She'd made it to

Arizona without him, hadn't she? She'd made it to thirty—thirty-two?—without him, hadn't she?

Offering to take her to dinner wasn't the smartest thing he'd done lately. The best thing he could do was get it over with, then take her back to the campground and forget about her.

"How wonderful!" Lit up like a Christmas tree, she squatted beside the river and scooped up a rock. Then, smiling like a child with a new puppy, she came back to where he was sitting and held it out for his inspection.

"It's a perfect heart," she said.

And it was. Beautifully sculpted by wind and water and time, the stone—deep red, shading to soft pink—seemed to come alive, as if she held someone's beating heart in the palm of her hand.

And maybe she did. Maybe she held his.

"I see," he said, knowing she expected more.

But that was all he was willing to give. Now and tomorrow and the day after that and all the days to follow.

He was used up, closed up, barricaded and immune to angels. He hoped.

Disappointment clouded her face, but she covered it quickly. Tucking the stone in her pocket, she smiled.

"Let's go eat," she said. "I'm hungry."

Once they'd settled back into the car, relief flooded Thunderhorse. His private torture was almost over. They'd eat, then he could go back to his camper where he could hole up, safe.

As he drove, Angel was silent for a while, the tranquillity of the river still with her. Then a sort of anxiousness settled over her.

"Is this restaurant we're going to well-known?"

"Only by the locals."

She seemed to ponder for a moment, then turned to him once more, her body tense with agitation.

"Will lots of people be there?"

Suddenly he knew the source of her distress. Because of her fame, Angel was considered public property. People would want to speak to her, get her autograph, even touch her. He pictured how it must be for her, a small fragile woman caught in the press of an eager crowd.

He noticed that her hands twisted tightly together in her lap. He almost reached over and covered them with his own. A last-minute attack of good sense saved him.

"I'll take care of you." He spoke tersely, his jaw tense, his eyes glued to the road.

"Thank you."

"You're welcome."

Thank God it was getting almost too dark to see her face. The lights of Montezuma Mama's pierced the night. He cruised the parking lot, looking at tags. No out-of-state ones. That was a good sign. Over the years Thunderhorse had discovered that the locals had little or no interest in outsiders. Live and let live seemed to be their motto, and as far as he was concerned it was a damned good one.

"Looks safe enough," he said.

"Good."

He liked that. A woman of few words. He smiled at the irony. In print, Angel Mercer was actually a woman of millions of words. Wasn't it always like that with writers? They spent so much energy pouring words into their books that they sometimes wanted to crawl into a hole of silence when they reentered the real world.

They made it through the restaurant door without incident. He walked beside her, not touching, but close just in case. He was vividly aware of how she came not quite up to his shoulder, of how, if he was holding her, he could rest his chin on top of her head.

They almost made it to the table, then suddenly a middle-aged couple wearing hats with beaver tails descended on them, bent on making themselves known to Angel. Thunderhorse recognized the gleam in their eyes.

"Brace yourself," he told her. "Here it comes."

She looked up, and the sheer impact of her eyes almost stopped him in his tracks. No wonder the fans couldn't get enough of her.

Neither would he...if he cared about her...if she belonged to him.

The man already had his camera poised, and the woman was barreling ahead, waving a hand loaded with at least five carats of diamonds.

"Yahoo," she called. "Angel—over this way." A flashbulb popped, and she whirled on her husband. "Not yet, you jerk. Wait till I get up there beside her."

"I don't think I can stand any more of this," Angel whispered. Her eyes were pleading.

Pure animal instinct took over. Thunderhorse scooped Angel up and marched back to the front door with her. Heads turned. People gasped. The diamond-draped matron yelled, "Quick, Harold, get a picture of that!"

Angel hid her face against his chest. Flashbulbs exploded. Somebody came from the kitchen yelling, "Hey, is that Angel Mercer?"

Thunderhorse kicked open the door and strode to the car.

"They got our picture," she said.

"It's all right."

"You can put me down now."

He jerked open the door and plopped her on the seat with more force than he intended, then raced around the car, climbed in and started the engine.

"Thanks," she said. "I didn't mean to be testy."

"No problem." A sense of loss swept over him, loss for the easy camaraderie of the early evening, loss for her smile, loss for things he dared not name.

His voice softened. "Everything's going to be all right."

He wished he believed what he was saying.

They didn't speak again until they were five miles down the road.

"Are you still hungry?" he asked.

"Yes."

"I know a place that makes the best western omelet this side of the Mississippi."

"Where?" Her skepticism showed. And her fear.

"My place." He glanced at her profile. "Unless you don't want to go there."

Stillness such as hers couldn't be described. She was like a small bird trapped in a cage, a forlorn kitten lost in an alley, a beautiful woman with no place to hide.

"I'll make an omelet and bring it over to your camper," he said, more sharply than he'd intended. Feeling rejected and out of sorts and more than a little confused.

"No. It's all right. I didn't mean to offend you."

"No problem."

Thunderhorse felt her hand settle on his—a dewdrop, an angel wing, a butterfly kiss.

"I'm sorry," she whispered. "It's not you. I was still thinking about those horrible people back at the restaurant."

"There were no out-of-state tags in the parking lot. They must be visiting relatives."

Silence. She turned her face to the window, and the moonlight gleamed in her hair. Impossibly bright. Impossibly soft and silky.

Thunderhorse wanted to touch her. He wanted to as much as he'd ever wanted anything in his life.

His hands tightened on the steering wheel.

"Thank you for the invitation." Her voice was so soft he had to lean toward her to hear. "I'll come to your place...for eggs."

Yes, he thought, for eggs. He'd have to remember that. The campground was just up ahead.

"I'd like to change first," she said. "If you don't mind."

"I don't mind."

While she was in her camper, Thunderhorse picked up a pair of boots in the middle of his floor and tossed them into the closet. Then he spotted a shirt he'd left hanging over the back of a chair, a dirty coffee cup making a stain on the table, a pair of socks hiding behind the broom.

He was getting to be a slob. He'd have to watch that. That was the danger of living alone.

Living alone. He wasn't going to think about that too much—and about all it meant.

There was a knock on the door and he said, "Come in." Suddenly Angel was standing in his living room wearing white, and Thunderhorse completely lost his breath. The dress was old-fashioned, high-necked and floor-length, made of some kind of fabric that looked like clouds, soft and billowy and sheer. Almost.

God, he could see the outlines of her legs through the skirt, impossibly long legs, slender, well toned, touchable, kissable. Her waist was no bigger than a handspan, and her breasts pushed lightly against the fabric in the most enticing way—in a way that could make a man lose his head.

And his tongue.

"I'm starving," she said.

"So am I," he said, but food was the furthest thing from his mind.

* * *

Angel was acutely aware of the way Thunderhorse was looking at her, and of the way his gaze made her feel. Feminine. Beautiful. Desirable.

Her skin heated, giving it a fine sheen that her grandmother used to refer to as a healthy glow. "Southern ladies never sweat, Angel," she would say. "We glow. Remember that. And always remember to be a lady."

Of course, being a lady was the furthest thing from Angel's mind right now. With this impossibly sexy Sioux looking at her with such raw hunger, what Angel had on her mind would make her grandmother roll over in her grave.

She was feeling things she'd never felt before, and oh, Lord, they felt so fine. Like flying. Like having shooting stars in your chest. Like celebrating Christmas every day of the year.

Was that why she'd worn the white dress? She'd bought it at a little boutique down on the Gulf coast because it reminded her of the kind of dress her grandmother might have worn as she walked along the beach, the sand squishing through her toes, the wind billowing her skirt and ruffling her hair. It reminded Angel of a slower-paced, more gracious era when people took the time to sit on their front porches and enjoy the sunsets, when they took the time to walk down the street after dinner and say hello to the neighbors, when they took the time to actually sit down at dinner and carry on a full-length conversation.

"You're an old-fashioned girl, Angel," her father was always telling her, and she guessed that was the truth.

Deep down all she really wanted was to love and be loved. That simple. That powerful.

Dan had said he loved her, and so had Britt, but she'd never told them the same thing. Couldn't bring herself to say the words. Couldn't even bring herself to think the words.

Now, standing in the trailer in the middle of Arizona

looking into the dark eyes of Thunderhorse and feeling her blood heat to the boiling point, Angel knew why. She hadn't loved them.

But she had fallen for them so quickly. So very quickly. Her past rose up to haunt her, and suddenly she was filled with sadness. Were her friends right? Did she need a watchdog?

When Thunderhorse said, "Won't you sit down?" she chose a chair as far away from him as possible.

Not that it made any difference. He was as glorious from a distance as he was up close.

She didn't know how she could endure the evening without doing something foolish, such as unbuttoning his shirt and running her hands down his fabulous chest, for she had not a single doubt that every inch of him was fabulous.

He continued to watch her, silent, and she held her breath, waiting. A small popping sound shattered the silence, and she could swear it was the sound of her skin sizzling.

"Bugs," he said. "They fly into the windows at night."

"I'm glad you warned me."

"Are you afraid, Angel?"

Afraid of what? That he would touch her? That he wouldn't touch her?

"No."

"Good."

Those black eyes, eating her up, inch by inch. She shivered.

He turned his back to her then and got busy at the stove. Still he didn't talk and neither did she. There was something in the room that didn't need words. Something electric.

Soon the delicious smells of frying onion and red peppers filled the air, and Angel had to put her hand over her stomach to contain the rumble. While she was dressing, she'd thought she was too tired to eat. But she was ravenous after all. And wide-awake.

"It's ready," he said, sooner than she expected, and the sound of his voice made her jump.

He served the omelets on sturdy pottery plates with distinctive Native American designs. They sat across from each other, too close for comfort, knees almost touching. But there was no help for it. After all, they were dining in a camper. When you travel, carrying your house with you, everything gets pared down.

"Delicious," she said, looking straight at his mouth.

"I'm glad you like it," he said, unable to take his eyes off hers.

"Oh, I do. Very much."

She'd never before noticed how a man's jaw could send out such strong signals. Power and strength and enormous sex appeal.

Her skin was tingling with heat again. Could he tell what she was thinking? She looked quickly down at her plate. Best to finish her dinner, then leave.

When she was done she said, "I'll help with the dishes."

"No. I'll do them later."

They both stood at the same time, so close her skirt brushed his leg and his upper arm touched hers. She was tempted to lean on him. Very tempted.

"I hate to eat and run, but I've been traveling for five days and suddenly I'm very tired."

"No problem."

"Thank you for the wonderful meal. I enjoyed it so much."

"Thank you."

Thank you for what? For coming? For eating eggs? For going home so he wouldn't have to play rescuer anymore?

Oh, Lord, she was getting punchy. It really was time to leave.

He was looking at her the way a man who wants to kiss a woman looks. Angel was certain of it. And she wanted him to kiss her. She wanted it more than anything she could remember wanting in her entire life.

And yet…she barely knew him. Then there was that ugly incident at the restaurant. And her awful past.

She had no reason to kiss him and a thousand to leave.

"Goodbye." She held out her hand. "And thanks for everything."

"You're welcome."

His clasp was brief, impersonal. He couldn't see her leave fast enough. There was no mistaking it. Thunderhorse wanted her out of his camper.

Probably out of his life. After all, she'd been nothing but trouble to him.

At the door she turned. "I'll write you a check tomorrow that should cover the damage."

He nodded. Was it in agreement? In disagreement? In dismissal?

She was too tired to think about it. Tomorrow would be soon enough to wonder.

Thunderhorse sat in the dark staring at Angel's camper. She'd left a night-light burning. If he looked hard enough, he could imagine he saw her stretched out on her bed, one arm slung over her head, her hair fanned golden across the pillow, one long leg out from under the white sheet.

He could make no sense of the day, none whatsoever. In less than twelve hours a mere slip of a woman had undone what it had taken him nine years to do: build a wall around himself.

She could never pay for the damage. It was already done, and he wasn't certain it could ever be undone.

Chapter Five

Thunderhorse was already gone when she awoke. She knew it immediately, without even looking across at his camper. A forlorn feeling settled over her, the sort she always got when she emerged from her office and found that she was entirely alone in the house, that Kaki and her father, in deference to her work, had totally deserted her. Sometimes they were merely in the garden walking arm in arm, or down the street at the university browsing through the library, or at the supermarket picking up cheese and crackers. But always, Angel knew she was alone.

Just as she did now.

Still, she peered out her window, just in case. His door was shut and his car was gone.

She ate a bird-size portion of cereal and banana, then found the phone near the campground entrance. She'd slept late. It was already ten o'clock back home, eleven in New York.

She called home first. "Kaki, it's Angel."

"Where are you?"

"Broken Arrow, Arizona."

"You made it."

"Didn't you think I would?" Her defensiveness showed, but she didn't care.

Instead of answering her, Kaki said, "How are you?"

"Fine."

That was the first flat-out lie she'd ever told to Kaki. Since she'd met Thunderhorse, she might never be fine again. Not in the way she'd always been, not in the way of having that most private part of herself untouched.

"Everything's great here," Kaki said. "Don't you worry about a thing. Just have a good time."

"Any important messages?"

"Just Britt. He's called three times wanting to know where he can reach you. Shall I give him your number?"

"No." Was her answer too quick? Too abrupt? "Tell him I need this time alone, Kaki. *Completely* alone."

"He's not going to like that. You know how he worries about you."

"I've no doubt that you can handle him, Kaki.... Now what about the benefit? Is Dad driving you crazy yet?"

Kaki laughed. "Almost. In the last three days he's decided to have a three-ring circus, a performance of *Aida* and a prom."

"What are we going to do with him?"

"Pamper him."

For a minute Kaki sounded almost soft. "Put him on," Angel said.

"How's my sweetheart?"

"You sound wonderful, Dad. Hale and hearty. Are you taking care of yourself?"

"Kaki's got me on a routine that would make a twenty-year-old faint. She's walking my tail off."

"Sounds as if that's exactly what you need."

"I'll have to admit, our early-morning walks are putting some bounce in my step. And how about you, darling? Are you enjoying the wild and woolly West?"

"It's fabulous. And, Dad, I saw a real Wild West Show. I wish you could have seen it."

"I do, too. Take care of yourself, darling."

"You, too, Dad."

Next, Angel called her agent.

"What are you doing calling me?" Jenny said. "You're supposed to be having a good time."

"I am."

"Then what are you doing wasting time on the telephone? Get out and kick up your heels, girlfriend."

"Jenny…somebody snapped my picture last night at the restaurant. Have you seen anything?"

"Nothing. Was it somebody you know? That idiot from the *Tribune* sneaking around in disguise?"

"No. They looked like a couple of ordinary tourists."

"Probably were. Don't give it another thought. Besides, it wouldn't be the first time an unauthorized picture of you got spread all over the newspaper."

"It's not myself I'm worried about."

"You were with somebody?"

"Not exactly."

"Not exactly. What in the hell does that mean?"

"Exactly what I said. I wasn't *with* anybody…just Thunderhorse."

"Wow. What a fabulous name. It sounds vaguely familiar. Did you make it up?"

"No. It's real. He's real."

"You should use that name in your next book."

"*Jenny*. This is serious."

"Okay. Look, if I get wind of anybody with outlaw photos of you and this Thunderhorse, I'll try to put the kibosh on it. What were you doing in that picture, anyway?"

"Nothing. I mean, not deliberately. I saw those people and freaked, and he picked me up and carried me out."

"Wow."

"Jenny, did I ever tell you that you have a limited vocabulary?"

"Many times, darling. Do you think I give a hoot? As long as we keep making each other rich, I'm happy."

"You have dollar signs for eyes. Some friend."

"Yeah, ain't I the limit? Bye, darling. Take good care of yourself, though it sounds like that's exactly what you're doing with this Thunderhorse. God, I can just picture him."

"Jenny…"

Angel's protest fell on deaf ears.

The line was already dead.

She glanced at her watch. It was almost time for Thunderhorse's show. Not that she was going. She had lots to do—explore the museums, look for art galleries, search out the Native American ruins, find a ghost town. The West was filled with exciting places to go and interesting things to see.

Of course, there was the matter of the check she'd promised Thunderhorse. She had to find out his first name, didn't she? Besides, who knew when she'd see him again? He might be leaving tomorrow. Or maybe she'd be.

Wouldn't it be better all around to take care of that little business matter before she forgot about it? The writer's curse. Absentmindedness. She was blessed with it, in spades.

She would definitely go to see his show. But not looking like a refugee from Camp Hopeless. Why not wear something pretty? After all, she always tried to look her best when she was conducting business.

She was not in the audience. Thunderhorse scanned the crowd again, looking for silky blond hair, a pair of the bluest eyes this side of heaven, a smile like no other he'd ever seen.

Fool, he chided himself. There was no reason Angel Mercer would come to his show again. And he should be damned glad she didn't. It would behoove him to concentrate on his rope tricks and quit acting like some besotted teenager.

He hadn't been this bad with Emily, even in the early days when their relationship was fresh, before everything went bad. For an instant, Emily flashed before his mind, dark eyes shining, mouth open in the laugh he used to love.

Did she ever laugh now? Probably not. What was there left to laugh about?

Pain slashed him, but he forced the memories aside. He had a show to do, an audience to please, a horse to ride.

He motioned for Shadow to come onstage, and just as the white stallion emerged from behind the curtain, Angel Mercer stepped into the big top.

Suddenly there was nothing but Angel, no show, no audience, no big top, just this exquisite woman wearing another of those diaphanous dresses that made Thunderhorse think of gas lamps and horse-drawn carriages and waxy white flowers perfuming the moonlit air.

Her dress was pink, the color of sweet summer sherbet, a soft summer sunrise. Hesitant, she stood in the doorway backlit by the sun, a tentative smile on her lips, a rosy flush spreading across her cheeks, a hat with a ribbon dangling from her hands.

It was time for the music, time for the dance. Never taking his eyes from her, Thunderhorse signaled for the music. Different music this time, music appropriate for the mood.

As the strains of Gershwin's "Embraceable You" filled the tent, Thunderhorse mounted his white stallion and rode straight to her.

"May I have this dance?"

"Yes."

He leaned down and scooped her onto the stallion, and the crowd went wild.

So did he. He tightened his arms around her, drawing her so close that every inch of her back was pressed solidly against him. Engulfed by her scent, crazed by it, he leaned forward and buried his lips in her hair.

"Oh, my." Her voice was a whisper, a sigh, an invitation.

"Yes," he said.

Shadow danced, the audience cheered, the music played on.

"I never dreamed of anything like this," she said.

Nor had he. His heart was a war drum, his blood a river a fire. Need, primal and raw, overrode reason.

Nothing existed except this moment and this woman.

Looking toward the control booth, Thunderhorse gave the wrap-up signal. Wayne Gatlin, his righthand man, lifted his eyebrows in astonishment, but he knew better than to question the boss. He dimmed the lights and faded the music while Thunderhorse and his Angel galloped out of the tent.

She swiveled to look at him. "What about the show?"

"The show's over."

"I'm glad," she said, then settled back against him as if riding off into the blazing sun with a slightly crazed Sioux was an everyday occurrence.

Thunderhorse guided the stallion past the parking lot, past the cars, past the ribbon of highway and beyond. In the distance lay his destination—a tall red spire, layer upon layer of rock shaped by years of sun and wind and rain.

Shadow's hooves thundered as they left civilization behind. Flying across the high-desert country with Angel's skirt streaming in the wind, Thunderhorse didn't think beyond the moment. As his ancestors had done before him, he became one with the land.

Burning with his unholy fire, he carried Angel deep into the canyons, through narrow passes, up steep grades, around serpentine curves. Every inch of it wild and primitive. Every inch of it unfamiliar to her.

And yet, she never questioned, never tensed. For all her ease, she might have been taking a horse-drawn carriage through Central Park. As they rode more deeply into the canyons, walls of polished rock rose around them, and in the distance they could hear the thundering of a waterfall.

"Look up, Angel." Thunderhorse reined Shadow to a halt so she could get a good look.

Two hundred feet up, perched atop a spire, was an eagle's nest. Circling above it was one of the most magnificent sights in high-desert country—an American bald eagle, soaring on wings that looked capable of taking him straight to the sun.

She shaded her eyes, then lost her breath as she spotted the eagle.

"He looks so…free."

"He is."

"It must be wonderful."

The wistful quality of her voice tore at his heart, and he wondered what price she had paid for fame. Once he'd paid the price and it had been far, far too high.

Using his knees and the gentle pressure of his hands, Thunderhorse guided the stallion farther into the canyon until the sound of the waterfall drowned out the sound of hooves. When they came to the last steep curve and the narrow passageway that would take them to paradise, he dismounted. Not for safety reasons, but because he wanted to see Angel's face.

She made a move to dismount, but he put a hand on her leg.

"Stay. Don't worry, I'll lead you safely in."

"I trust you."

"Close your eyes.... Ready?"

"Yes."

They went through the doorway of rock, and it was like stepping back in time. As always, Thunderhorse stood for a moment in silent awe. Cathedral-like, the rocks rose in polished splendor, and the sun created a pattern of light and shadow that fell across the natural grotto like a benediction. Water tumbled in a free fall over the rocks, thundering into the clear pool at their base. Native plants, untrampled by man, lent a lushness that was surprising in the ancient canyon.

Angel put her hands over her heart, overcome, and tears glistened in her eyes.

"It's the most incredibly beautiful thing I've ever seen," she whispered.

Thunderhorse thought his heart would burst.

"I wanted to give you the world."

A tear slid from the corner of her eye and glistened on her cheek.

"You did. Thank you."

She stretched out her arms and he lifted her off the horse. A breeze caught her hair and her dress billowed against his legs. Her feet touched the ground, but she held on, hands around his neck, arms over his shoulders.

The past twenty-four hours coalesced into one shining moment, and the kiss they shared stopped the universe. The power of the waterfall was in it and the heat of the sun, the tenderness of the deep green pool and the promise of the enduring earth.

They kissed until they lost their breaths, and then they held on to each other, swaying in a rhythm as old as time, as suggestive as an erotic dance.

He could feel her heartbeat, see the blush on her cheeks, smell the mingled scents of her perfume and a skin on fire.

"I don't want to ever leave this place," she whispered.

"Nor do I."

He took her hand and led her to the water, and she pulled off her shoes to wade in the shallow, the hem of her dress dragging in the water and the ribbon that dangled from her hat getting wet. He smiled and she laughed, kicking water at him.

He waded in, moccasins and all, and they played chase like two naughty children. He caught her in midstream and kissed her again. Then, because the sun was beating down, he took the hat from her hand and placed it tenderly atop her golden hair.

She turned his hand over and kissed his palm.

"You're sweet," she said.

"I'm many things, but sweet is not one of them."

"You're wrong. You're very sweet and tender."

She almost made him believe it was true.

"You don't know me."

"I know you, Thunderhorse. It only takes a moment to see a person's soul."

"Your innocence clouds your vision."

"I'm not innocent."

"Yes, you are."

The wind threatened her hat, but she clamped it down, then leaned back to gaze up at him.

"Is this our first argument?"

He laughed. "No. I refuse to argue on the day I gave you the world."

Standing on tiptoe, she kissed him, then danced away, laughing, the ribbons whipping around her face.

"In movies they stand behind the falls," she said. "Is that possible?"

"Sometimes."

"Here? Now?" Her expression was as eager as a child's.

"Yes." He took her hand. "Hold on tight."

"I won't let go."

He didn't want her to. Ever. Something soft and magical stole into his heart, and for a moment he believed it was possible that one special woman could tumble walls and create miracles.

They waded until the water reached waist deep on her, then he lifted her in his arms and carried her the rest of the way. Sure of his footing, he bore her toward the roaring curtain of water.

Droplets rained on them, and she stuck her tongue out to catch them.

"The water tastes wild," she said.

In one word she had captured captured the essence of the canyon. *Wild.* And with that wildness, freedom.

Guided by instinct and the feel of rock through the soles of his moccasins, he climbed a natural stairway that led through the falls. Viewed through the crystal curtain, the world softened, colors merged, and rainbows shot from the sky—double, then triple until the entire grotto shimmered.

Hair drooping, clothes wet and clinging, Angel lifted her face to his. "I think I've found heaven."

Today was a gift from the universe, and against all his better judgment, he took it.

Thunderhorse tightened his hold on her. "So have I."

Chapter Six

With the roar of the waterfall filling the canyon, Angel reached for Thunderhorse's hand. It seemed so natural, holding his hand, standing in companionable silence with him, trusting him.

I won't analyze this, she told herself. I won't think about the past and why I've never felt this way before. I'm just going to let myself *be*.

It was cool behind the curtain of water, and when she shivered Thunderhorse immediately picked her up and carried her back to the shore. Then, without a word he got his saddle blanket and spread it on the ground for her.

She smiled at him, sat, then closed her eyes, leaned back and tipped her face to the sun. She could feel him sitting beside her, feel the heat of his body, his solid reassuring presence.

Was this what it was like for her parents? She used to watch them sitting on the porch swing, hands clasped, rocking gently, sometimes talking in low murmurs, sometimes merely enjoying their closeness and the quietness of the evening.

She'd always been slightly disappointed that she couldn't capture that certain something she'd seen in her parents. Strange that although she was a writer, she couldn't put a name to it. And stranger still that it was the moment she stopped looking for it that she found it. Here. Now. In this remote canyon with a quiet man who was almost a stranger to her.

Almost.

Eyes still closed, she reached for his hand and suddenly it was there, big and strong and oh-so-comforting. And she wondered why people didn't hold hands anymore. She wondered why books and movies showed love as passionate kisses and lots of naked skin in the dark, but ignored the simple pleasure of holding hands.

Lulled by happiness and the warmth of the sun, Angel nodded and might have fallen asleep, but Thunderhorse put her hat back on her head.

"You're very fair. You'll burn quickly."

Even sitting, he looked tall…and enduring, like the bluffs beyond.

"You're a gentle giant, did you know that?"

"Only two people have ever referred to me as gentle."

"Who were they?"

Thunderhorse simply shut down. That was the only way Angel could describe it. One minute he was sitting beside her, face and heart and soul wide open, and the next he was closed up as tightly as a bank vault.

"That was a nosy question," she said. "I withdraw it."

"We have to go back. I have another show to do."

The ride out of the canyon was very different from the ride in. For one thing, the silence thundered around them, dark, restless and filled with a million questions. For another, she didn't feel comfortable leaning against him anymore. It felt like leaning against a bag full of explosives.

She had been foolish and irresponsible. After all, what did she know of this man? That he'd helped her park her camper, that he'd rescued her in the restaurant, that he was a beautiful performer with a way with a horse—and a way with women. Especially her.

He could be a con man. Or worse. He could be another Dan Calloway.

Here she was, a celebrity, not by choice, but a celebrity nonetheless. And wealthy. The whole world knew what she was worth, thanks to the media. Nothing was sacred to them.

Anything could happen to her out here. If she ever got back to her car, she was going to act with a little more gumption. She would go sight-seeing—on Jeep tours with lots of people—and look at galleries and go shopping and maybe, just maybe, venture into a really good restaurant or two. She wasn't a very good cook and she was tired of her own cooking.

As a matter of fact, she might just sell her camper and fly to a resort where she would hole up in a nice big hotel that had bathtubs as big as Texas and very good room service.

Loss settled around her heart, and she looked over her shoulder to see the canyon, but all she saw was some sagebrush and a jackrabbit.

She sighed. It was hard to lose paradise.

The big top hove into view, and Thunderhorse drew the stallion to a halt beside her car. She slid off.

"Thanks for a lovely day." She held her hand up to him, and for a moment she thought he was going to kiss it.

Instead, he said, "You're welcome," then rode in the direction of his Wild West Show without even looking back.

"He didn't even ask me to stay for the show," she said to no one.

Tears stung her eyelids when she climbed into her hot car. As she drove off, she wondered who he would pick to be his dance partner, and whether he would signal the soundman to play "Embraceable You."

"I hope she has buck teeth and bad breath."

Having said that, Angel wiped her face with the back of her hand, then headed in the direction she hoped was town. She was going shopping and she was going to spend an obscene amount of money.

"It's a surefire cure for the blues," Jenny always said.

Angel was willing to try anything.

Thunderhorse was in a foul mood. The minute he was inside the big top, he found Wayne Gatlin.

"I'm cutting Shadow's dance out of the show this afternoon."

"Is there a problem with the stallion?"

"No."

Wayne didn't generally argue with Thunderhorse, but today he made an exception.

"Then I don't understand why you're cutting it out. That's everybody's favorite part of the show."

"I'll add a few rope tricks."

Wayne started to protest again, but the look on Thunderhorse's face changed his mind.

"Whatever you say."

"How's the crowd?"

"Slim."

"Good. This will be our last show."

"I thought you were doing them through next week."

"Winter's coming early this year. It's time to end the show and head home."

"You won't get any argument from me on that. I'll be glad to get back to the ranch. Will you be heading back tonight?"

Thunderhorse thought of Angel, alone on the campground.

"No."

"If it's all right by you, I'm leaving as soon as the big top's down and the equipment's packed."

"I'll pack up. You head on after the show, and when you get to the ranch, tell Lucas I'll be there in a few days."

Not that Lucas Gray Wolf needed to be told anything. Not only was he the best rancher in Arizona, he was the best friend a man could have. Thunderhorse would trust his life to Lucas.

And had, once, but that was a memory Thunderhorse tried to ignore. Along with a thousand other memories.

Today he'd added another. Angel. The touch of her lips would haunt him forever.

He snatched his costume off the rack and transformed himself to Sitting Bull. He wished such transformations were as easy on the inside as they were on the outside.

Angel gave her name as Sally Williams in honor of her favorite playwright, Tennessee Williams, who was actually a native Mississippian, though most folks thought he was born in Tennessee.

Nobody in the Arizona Jeep Tour questioned her, and she was feeling triumphant about her coup when all of a sudden the woman sitting in front of her turned around and shouted, "Omigod, it's Angel Mercer! Omigod, I love your books. Muriel is my all-time favorite character. How in the world did you ever think of her?"

At least she didn't whip out a camera. Nor did anybody else. Angel didn't mind talking about her work to perfect strangers. Not really. It just wasn't something she wanted to talk about all the time.

"It's magic," she said, hoping that would suffice. "The whole writing process."

"Yes, but didn't you have a friend or something by the name of Muriel? Didn't I read that somewhere?"

"It was my mother's middle name."

"I'm dying to know what Muriel will be doing next. Can you give me a hint?"

Angel felt the bars of her cage closing in. Besides that, she was missing all the petroglyphs.

"Honey—" the woman's husband plucked at her sleeve "—she's here on tour, just like us."

"Ohhh...sorry."

"No problem."

Nobody else asked Angel any questions. Still, the incident was enough to send her to the grocery store in search of something to cook for dinner rather than to one of the enticing-looking restaurants she passed on the way into town.

She got a steak. Who could go wrong with steak?

Angel was late getting home.

Thunderhorse paced, glancing out the windows every time he passed. It was already dark. What could be keeping her?

"None of your damned business," he told himself, then turned to the stove to cook a very good ranch stew. He should have gone home this afternoon, as Wayne had. *There* was a man with plenty of common sense.

His stew bubbled and simmered, and Thunderhorse glanced anxiously out the window. What if she'd run into trouble again? He'd seen how quickly eager fans could turn to dangerous mobs.

"Fool."

He jerked a bowl out of the cabinet. What made him think he could be her protector? He'd failed miserably at that job once. Hadn't he learned his lesson?

The lights of her car cut through the darkness. Thunderhorse filled his bowl with stew, then sat with his back to the window.

What Angel Mercer did was no concern of his.

She was singing when she got out of her car, singing well, too, a nice clear soprano. Listening, Thunderhorse almost choked on his stew.

The song was "Embraceable You."

Was she remembering, too? He was glad when the door slammed and she was safely inside her camper. She could sing like a bird now and it didn't matter. Thunderhorse couldn't hear.

He would definitely go home tomorrow. Early. Right after sunrise. Maybe before. Before Angel woke up.

He washed his bowl, keeping his back staunchly toward the windows, then picked up the latest legal thriller. That ought to keep his mind off his next-door neighbor.

On page twenty-five he thought he smelled something burning. By page thirty-five he was absolutely certain.

Putting his book down, Thunderhorse lifted his head and sniffed. Charred steak. There was nothing else in the world that smelled like it.

Angel was burning dinner.

He opened his book once more, but page thirty-six made no sense. He read it three times before he gave up.

The smells wafting across the space between their campers were stronger. Furthermore, smoke drifted past his window.

Thunderhorse had to look. There was no help for it.

Angel stood at her open window, fanning smoke with a dish towel.

''Need any help?'' was on the tip of his tongue. He bit it back just in time.

Who in the hell was he to offer help?

He tossed his book aside, then settled down with his guitar. He was self-taught and not very good, but learning a few new chords seemed to be the best thing to keep his mind off the woman next door.

He plucked away, hitting some very sour notes. His conscience smote him. Here he was, fed and comfortable, with a big pot of leftovers, while Angel had obviously burned her dinner and—if he knew her—didn't have a thing to eat.

''Not my problem,'' he said, and that selfish attitude lasted all of three minutes.

Before he knew it, he was filling a bowl with stew and knocking on her door. He was absolutely certain he would live to regret it.

Chapter Seven

Angel was so mad when she saw Thunderhorse standing at her door that she could have hit him with her dishrag. Who did he think he was, dismissing her like a pile of dirty laundry, then showing up at her door? The Prince of Wales?

"Hello, there," he said, as if he hadn't kissed her till her toes curled this afternoon, then left her standing in a hot parking lot without a backward glance.

"What do you want?"

He was taken aback by her sharp tone. Well, good for him. Good for her. Her kitchen was filled with smoke, she didn't have any dinner, and she had come within an inch of burning her camper down around her head.

She had a right to be angry.

"I thought you might like some stew."

The most delicious fragrance arose from the bowl he was holding in her direction that she almost swooned with delight. Fortunately she had more self-control.

She had no intention of swooning over anything Thunderhorse did. Ever again.

"No, thank you," she said, as polite as could be. She wasn't born in the South for nothing. Southern girls had manners. Most of the time.

She was happy to see that she'd rendered him speechless again. Furthermore, he looked distinctly uncomfortable, such a big man holding such a tiny bowl.

Good. She hoped he stayed that way all night. She hoped he didn't get a lick of sleep. It would serve him right.

"Why don't I leave it here in case you change your mind?"

"Whatever you like."

She held the door open, then stepped back as far as she could. She wasn't about to touch him. Or his bowl, either.

He set the bowl on her table, then stood with the smoke swirling around his head and the smell of burned steak offending his nostrils. Before she could tell him to stop, he was flinging open windows and turning on the fan over the stove.

"I was going to do that."

She was furious that she hadn't thought of it. And wouldn't have thought of it in a million years. Writers didn't belong in a world of gadgets. So many darned things to twist and turn on and punch in and log on. The things that set out to foil her boggled her mind. Her computer, for instance. It was always gobbling her manuscripts and zapping off into outer space.

And e-mail. On the information highway, she was a pothole. Didn't people talk to people anymore?

She preferred face-to-face conversations. Except not Thunderhorse's face. And not now.

"Thank you for coming."

She wasn't going to forget her upbringing, even if it killed her to be polite.

"Are you dismissing me?"

"No, I said thank you, just as polite as could be."

"It wasn't what you said, it was the way you said it. Your tone of voice would freeze beer."

"What are you all of a sudden—Mr. Manners?"

Thunderhorse just looked at her, but such a look. It was fraught with a million unspoken thoughts. It was the kind of look that compelled her to talk, even when she had vowed to be remote and silent.

"When I'm escorted somewhere by a man, I don't expect to be dropped off in a hot parking lot without so much as a goodbye, thanks for a nice day, be seeing you around sometime. You just dumped me, then rode off like some Sioux Sphinx."

"Sioux Sphinx?"

His eyes twinkled and his mouth quirked at the corners.

"If you laugh at me, I'm going to throw something. Hard."

"I'm not laughing at you."

He closed the distance between them before she was even aware that he had moved. Then suddenly he was kissing her.

Such a kiss. The kind that moved mountains, called down the rains and made the sun stand still. She felt as if she was caught up in the middle of a hurricane.

All she could do was catch the front of his buckskin shirt and hang on. It was like clinging to the Rock of Gibraltar. That solid. That safe. That good.

She could have stayed in his arms for the next century or two.

When the kiss ended, he cupped her face and tipped it upward.

"Good night, Angel. Thanks for a nice day. I'll be seeing you around." At the door he turned back to her. "Eat your stew. You're going to need your strength."

What did he mean by that? She would need her strength to fight off rabid fans? To fight off him? To love him?

Through her open window she could hear him whistling. "Embraceable You." She would never again hear that Gershwin tune without thinking of Thunderhorse and his beautiful white stallion.

She listened until he was inside his camper, then she moved to her window so she could see him. He pulled his shirt off, as bold as you please. What was a girl to do?

She stayed at her window staring, fantasizing and lusting in her heart of hearts and every other part of her body that counted.

He picked up a guitar and started strumming. Was it the Gershwin tune? She wished his windows were open so she could hear.

She propped her elbows on the windowsill and let the soft night air cool her face. Tomorrow morning she was going to get up and cook eggs. It was impossible to ruin eggs.

Then she was going to invite Thunderhorse over for breakfast. After all, she still didn't know his first name.

Thunderhorse had meant to leave early, but how could he leave with Angel standing at the window wearing a blue ribbon in her hair?

Tomorrow would be soon enough to leave. Or the day after.

Whistling the Gershwin tune he couldn't get out of his mind, he picked up his skillet and was just going to start breakfast when he saw the car roaring through the gates of the campground. A black Mustang convertible. A man at the wheel. Alone.

And he was headed straight for Angel's camper.

If it was some pushy fan or equally pushy reporter, he was going to go over there and throw him out.

Couldn't they leave her alone? She deserved a vacation in peace, like ordinary people.

He was almost at the door when the man got out of the car. It was none other than Britt Ace. When he took off his sunglasses, Thunderhorse saw the blue eyes that made women all over America swoon. With his sun-burnished hair and cleft chin he was more movie idol than anchor of television's top-rated news show.

Surely a man of his stature wouldn't come all the way to Arizona unless he had a prearranged meeting with Angel. Still, with the members of today's press you never could tell.

Nine years ago it was different. Quickly he forced that line of thinking out of his head.

Then he tensed, waiting and watching. When Angel came to the door, her mouth dropped open in surprise.

That did it. Thunderhorse was going to put that interloper on the road. No matter who he was.

Thunderhorse had barely gained the door when the heart-throb of the late-night news swept America's bestselling novelist into his arms.

"Aren't you glad to see me, sweetheart?"

Sweetheart?

While he watched, Britt kissed Angel on the cheek. Thunderhorse didn't stay to see if she was pleased. Didn't want to see. Didn't want to know.

He eased back into his camper. He'd wasn't about to be caught spying.

His appetite gone, he flung the skillet back into the cabinet. Then he removed his boots and threw them across the room.

The burst of satisfaction was short-lived. He picked up a newspaper and jerked it open. A man had a right to read the news, didn't he?

No matter what was going on right under his nose.

Furthermore, he'd be damned if he would let Britt Ace drive him out. He was going to stay on this campground until he decided to leave.

Angel didn't know whether to laugh or cry. On the one hand, Britt was a welcome diversion. Thunderhorse had turned her entire world upside down. As her grandmother used to say, she didn't know whether she was coming or going.

On the other hand, Britt was a control-freak intruder, who had deliberately defied her wishes.

"My eggs are burning." She shoved at Britt's chest and was gratified with how quickly he let her go.

"How like you, Angel."

She whirled on him, furious. "Don't you take that condescending tone with me. I've had about enough of your high-handed manners, Britt Ace."

"That's a fine thanks I get for coming halfway across the country to see about you."

"Nobody asked you to come."

"I take it you're not thrilled to see me."

"I specifically asked you not to come."

"I don't take orders, Angel. You know that."

Britt couldn't even argue without still looking and acting as if he was in front of a television camera. His amiability made Angel furious.

"What would it take to ruffle your feathers, Britt?"

"I'm unflappable, my dear. That's part of my charm. You told me so yourself once."

"I changed my mind a long time ago about your charm, and you're treading on thin ice when it comes to friendship. Some friend you turned out to be." Angel dumped the eggs into the garbage can. "How did you find me, anyway?"

"I took the red-eye to Phoenix, then rented the flashiest car on the lot, and here I am. In living color and with sound."

The thing about Britt was that he could always make her laugh. She guessed that was why they'd remained friends after she broke the engagement.

"That's not what I meant, and you know it," she said.

"Jenny told me."

"So the two of you are in cahoots now."

"I'd as soon be in cahoots with a grizzly bear. She was worried about you, that's all. When she told me about that picture, I decided I'd better fly out here and take care of things."

"Take care of things? Just what do you mean by that?"

"Help you find a driver to take this piece of junk you call a camper home. You can fly back with me. I've been wanting to see your dad, anyhow. How is he?"

"Don't change the subject. For your information, I'm on vacation and I have no plans to leave, certainly not with you."

"If I weren't such a nice guy, I'd take that personally."

"Take it personally, Britt. You know why I broke the engagement and why Mae did the same thing two years later and why every other girl you date will do the same."

His reply was a slight lift of a perfectly groomed eyebrow. Angel hated that gesture.

"Because you're a control freak, that's why."

"Does this mean you're not flying back with me?"

"Haven't you heard a word I've said? Read my lips, Britt. I'm not going home."

Britt studied his perfectly groomed nails before impaling her with his laser-beam eyes.

"Does your decision have anything to do with that man in the picture Jenny told me about?"

Britt always had a nose for truth. And yet, Thunderhorse was only part of the reason she was staying. The rest of it had nothing to do with him or with anybody else. If she stayed it was just possible that she might slay a few dragons. If she stayed it was just possible that when she drove home she could go right through Texas, turning her head right and left to look at every single sagebrush and tumbleweed she encountered.

"This is not about him," she said. "I don't even know his first name."

He laughed. "Angel, you're constitutionally unsuited for subterfuge. That's one of the reasons I adore you." He kissed the tip of her nose. "All right. My flight doesn't leave till tomorrow morning. I'll play tourist and you play tour guide."

"There are some really good petroglyphs nearby."

"Then get your hat, my dear. I'm in a convertible, and you know how you burn in the sun."

Angel caught her breath. Another man had said that, another time, another place.

As she climbed into the car beside Britt, she glanced at the camper next door. Thunderhorse was nowhere in sight.

Chapter Eight

Thunderhorse felt as if two grizzlies were fighting inside his chest, and it didn't take a genius to figure out why. Even when he heard the fancy sports car leave early, even when he saw Angel standing in the door waving goodbye, even when he knew that Britt Ace was leaving without her, that still didn't alter the facts: He had spent the night with Angel.

The thing to do was leave the campgound. Immediately. The big top was dismantled. He'd done that yesterday. There was nothing to keep him from driving off and never looking back.

Nothing except Angel.

He jerked on his shirt, and before he could change his mind, he was standing at her camper, knocking on the door.

Angel was still in her robe when she heard the knock on her door. She flushed all over when she saw who it was.

"I hate to bother you so early in the morning," he said,

as polite as a stranger. As polite as if they'd never stood under a waterfall together, holding hands.

"No problem. I was up, anyway."

"May I?" He nodded toward the door, and she held it wider.

"Of course. Come in." It was amazing how some men merely occupied a room and how some filled it. With Thunderhorse inside, there seemed no way to turn without brushing against him.

"Coffee?" she said. Thank goodness Britt had made some before he left for the airport. "You always put too much coffee in the pot," he'd said, and since he'd been a model of tact once he found out she'd made up her mind to stay, she'd let that remark pass.

Thunderhorse was restless. She'd never seen him this way. He kept looking around the camper as if he expected to find gremlins hiding under the furniture.

She handed him the cup, careful not to linger over that brief touch. She stood beside him, loving his being there, loving his body heat, loving his solid strength. Stood too long with him holding on to his coffee cup and her barely holding on to her sanity.

"Won't you sit down?" Thankfully he did and she could breathe again. She cinched her robe tighter, stood behind the tiny bar that divided kitchen from living room.

"I just came over to tell you I'm leaving this morning."

Her heart sank. She hoped her disappointment didn't show.

"Well, then…I'll get your bowl. It's clean. I washed it last night."

"This is good coffee."

"Britt made it."

He set the cup down. Actually, *banged* was a better word.

She could tell by the squaring of his jaw that he wouldn't drink another drop.

"He's a TV anchor," she said.

"I know who he is."

The silence was deafening, the air charged. Angel could never stand long silences, and she hated the suspicion that had suddenly entered the room. Not that things had been going great between them, anyhow, but she had to try to explain.

"We were engaged once, but now we're just good friends."

The awful silence screamed around her, and she clutched the edge of the counter for support. Why was it so much easier for a writer to put words on paper than to speak them face-to-face?

"Look, I know what you're thinking, and that's absolutely not true."

"It's none of my business," he said.

That did it. If there was anything Angel hated, it was being dismissed as if nothing she said or did mattered. She flew around the counter, hands clenched, jaw jutted. She was in what her father called her clear-the-path mode.

"You're darned right it's none of your business. I happen to have lots of friends, and if one of them is a man, that doesn't mean I treat him any differently than how I treat my female friends. For your information, I slept on the bed and he slept on the couch."

"I didn't ask."

"Oh, yes, you did. You charged in here with those black eyes of yours darting every which way, seething with curiosity and...and jealousy."

"Jealousy?"

His voice was dangerously soft, but she ignored the warning signal. She always had. Damn the torpedoes and full speed ahead. That was her motto. It had gotten her into more trouble than she cared to think about.

"That's what I said. *Jealous*. You kiss me once and you think you own me. For your information, I can't be owned and I don't take orders."

"Once?"

Her blood was heating up. His was, too, if his expression was any indication. She pushed her hair off her flushed face.

"Well, maybe more than once."

It was wonderful and terrible, the way a determined man unfolded himself from a little chair. And when he stalked her, she felt as if she was in the middle of an earthquake. She grabbed the nearest chair and held on.

But she didn't retreat. She wasn't about to retreat.

"Here's one that you will remember," he said.

He knew that what he was about to do was foolhardy. But he could no more have stopped himself than he could stop the sun from rising in the east.

When he took her in his arms, she stiffened in resistance. That small defiance heated his blood to the boiling point. He stormed her defenses as fiercely as his ancestors had stormed forts.

The minute his lips touched hers, she went boneless, melting, melting into him, and he knew that he could never drive off and leave her behind. Never.

He had to have this woman. All of her. Heart, mind, body and soul. No matter what the cost.

She made a soft sound of surrender, and he lifted her off her feet, mouths sealed, bodies melded. He was holding the stars, the moon, the universe itself. The force of his passion shook him like a willow in the wind, and he stood in the middle of her camper, kissing her, devouring her, and swaying to the rhythm of some ancient tribal dance.

He wanted her as he never wanted another woman. All of her. But not here. Not now.

She was his Angel. With her everything had to be perfect. When he released her, she leaned her head against his chest, sighing.

"Come with me," he said.

"Yes."

She didn't even ask where. Thunderhorse felt ten feet tall.

Chapter Nine

Surrounded by pinnacles of sandstone and red rock and bordered by Coconino National Forest, Paradise Ranch took Angel's breath away.

"We're home," Thunderhorse said, and Angel knew it was true.

Never had she been in a place that called so fiercely to her soul. Never had she seen a place that felt as if she'd known it forever.

He caught her hand and lifted it to his lips.

"Welcome home, Angel."

Her spirits soared. With those two words Thunderhorse gave her everything she'd ever wanted—love, security, promise and a deep sense of well-being.

She was glad she'd let him talk her into riding with him, glad he'd said he would have someone pick up her camper later, glad she'd listened to her heart, instead of reason.

Light and shadow played across the canyon walls as

Thunderhorse lifted her from his camper. A pale sliver of moon floated in the darkening sky, and Venus was as bright as flame.

He carried her across the threshold, the vow they'd exchanged when he said, "Come with me," and she said yes, as binding as if they'd stood in a church before God and her entire family. A lamp glowed in the hallway, and she had a fleeting impression of dark paneling, of Oriental rugs on gleaming oak floors, of priceless antiques paired with heavy furniture upholstered in supple leather.

Like its owner, the house gave the impression of comfort and durability.

The staircase curved upward to the second floor, which was lit only by the moon gleaming through the wide windows. Even at night the vistas through the glass created the illusion of being outside, instead of in.

He kicked open a heavy carved door, then carried her to a bed that seemed to float in the middle of a moonlit room. It was enormous, with carved posts and a massive headboard. The spread was like thunderclouds, dark plush silver. She sank into the covers with a sigh, her white skirt flaring around her.

"You are so beautiful." Thunderhorse leaned over her, his eyes twin coals, searching, wanting, burning, *burning*.

She lifted her arms toward him. An invitation. A promise. And he covered her, careful to keep his weight on his elbows.

"I don't want to hurt you," he whispered. "Ever."

"You won't hurt me."

He prayed that was so. She looked fragile, breakable, lying in the middle of his bed; for an instant his past rose ghostlike in his mind, and he trembled in the grip of cold fear.

What if he failed this woman?

He could not, he must not, for to fail Angel would be to destroy himself, as well as her. The words he'd written nine years earlier haunted him: The greatest agony is not dying; it's living.

Agony. He'd been filled with it, consumed by it, paralyzed by it. And yet, there was a flip side.

Ecstasy. Angel had given him a glimpse of it, and with that glimpse, hope.

She touched his face, softly, tenderly.

"Thunderhorse."

"Yes?"

"I don't even know your name."

Trust shimmered in her eyes. And something else, something he could only call love.

"Steve," he said. "Steve is my name."

"Then come to me, Steve," she whispered. "Come to me."

Alight with passion, aching with desire, he reached for her buttons. Every atom in his body tensed as he started the slow unveiling.

Her skin was silver in the moonlight, soft and gleaming, impossibly lovely. Her dress shimmered as he slid it off her shoulders. She'd worn white, virginal bridal white, and he was glad.

It was symbolic. He would be her first, her only lover, and she would be his.

When she lay naked on his bed, he worshiped her with lips and fingers and tongue, every inch of her, starting at her slender throat and working his way down to her pink-tinted toenails. She was the most giving woman he'd ever had, the most responsive and by far the most appealing.

The fragrance of her skin was old-fashioned—damask roses. He used to raise them in his backyard in D.C. A lifetime ago. The heady scent was caught in her hair, in her soft silken curves.

With her hands tangled in his hair, her body taut and alive beneath him, he drank deeply of her.

"I want you, Steve," she whispered. "All of you."

She wrapped herself around him, cradled him with arms and legs. Deeply sheathed, he finally found peace. And hope. And a joy he'd never known.

His body soared, his heart exulted. *I love you. I love you.* Over and over the words tumbled through his mind, and yet he wouldn't say them aloud. Couldn't say them aloud.

To admit love was to be vulnerable. To admit love was to risk a hurt so deep and dark it had taken nine years to embrace the light.

And so he would not say the words to Angel. But he would show her. Oh, how he would show her.

Angel had never known such ecstasy. "This is the stuff of dreams," she whispered.

And he responded by taking her to new heights of joy, showing her new planes of pleasure. Every inch of her body came alive, tingled, exploded.

Sweat-slickened, he turned them over so that he lay flat against the covers, gorgeous and golden, his skin gleaming in the moonlight. He caught her hands, entwined their fingers, and she found paradise.

"Now I know what it's like to ride a Thunderhorse."

His laughter was rich and full and sexy, and drove her absolutely wild. Any lingering inhibitions she had flew out the window, and he encouraged her with murmurs of pleasure.

Changing patterns of light on the silver spread measured the journey of the moon. Angel's journey from aloneness to fulfillment was measured in the increasing intensity of her soft cries.

She was a comet streaking through the sky, a star exploding in space, a entire galaxy being born.

"Now, Steve," she cried. "Now."

And still he held her in thrall. Muscles corded in his neck and his arms, and suddenly he was speaking in the strange and beautiful language of his ancestors. Dark and musical, the words washed over her, through her, and her love for him overflowed.

"I love you," she whispered. "I love you."

Buried deep, he filled her as rain fills Mother Earth.

He pressed his damp forehead against her, and she lay in his arms, slack and soft and content.

And just before she drifted into sleep, she remembered that he hadn't said he loved her back.

Angel was still sleeping when Steve left his bed the next morning. Careful not to wake her, he pressed a tender kiss to her forehead, then dressed quietly and stole from the room.

He found Lucas at the barn, grooming the two-year-old filly they'd named Blazing Star. Lucas took one look at him and grinned.

"Need I ask what kept you so long?"

"No."

"I saw your camper this morning."

"Yep." Steve picked up a currycomb and began to groom the filly.

"Only a woman would keep you abed till midmorning."

"It's only six."

"Anybody I know?"

"No."

"You're going to make me drag this out of you, aren't you?"

"Yes."

Lucas threw down his brush, then pulled out his pipe and began tamping in tobacco, a sure sign that he wasn't about to give up until he had what he wanted.

"Okay, who is she and where did you meet her and how important is she to you?"

Wayne hadn't mentioned a thing about the beautiful blonde Thunderhorse had chosen as his dance partner two days in a row at the Wild West Show. Steve had known he wouldn't, but it was good to have that faith confirmed.

Not that he kept any secrets from Lucas. Never had and never would.

"It's Angel Mercer."

"Angel Mercer?"

"Yeah, one and the same. I met her at the Wild West Show, and she's very important to me. Too important."

Lucas puffed silently for a while, which was also his way as he processed and absorbed information. Then he put his hand on Steve's shoulder and squeezed.

"I'm glad," he said. "I was afraid it would never happen."

"So was I. But it did, and now I'm scared to death."

"I'm not one to advise on matters of the heart. Never ventured into that treacherous terrain and never plan to. All I can say is this—you're equal to any task, Steve. *Any task.* And don't you forget it."

Lucas picked up his brush and began to groom the filly, and Steve knew the discussion was over. He wouldn't ask any more questions, he wouldn't pry, he wouldn't prod.

Lucas Gray Wolf would do the one thing any loyal friend would: Whatever happened he would stand by Steve Thunderhorse.

* * *

The first thing Angel saw when she awoke was the bright sunlight filling the room, so bright she had to squint. The second was Steve, sitting on the edge of her bed, a breakfast tray in his hands.

"Good morning, sleepyhead." He kissed her softly. "Sleep well?"

"Mmm. Never better." She stretched, then looked at the tray. "You're spoiling me."

"Are you complaining?"

"Never." She picked up the orange juice and took a long swallow. "A girl could get used to this kind of treatment."

"That's the general idea."

She sat up, pulling the sheet with her. He spread a white linen napkin over her lap, then fed her bits of toast with honey, every now and then stopping to kiss the crumbs away.

"I can feed myself, you know."

"I know. But I'm having fun. How about you?"

"Absolutely."

She polished off her orange juice and the rest of the toast, then eyed the bowl of strawberries.

"I don't know that I can eat those."

"Those are for me." All innocence, he set the tray aside, then folded her napkin and set the berries on the bed. "I always did fancy a little midmorning snack."

"They look delicious." She reached for one, but he gently slapped her hand away.

"They will be, believe me." The way he looked at her made her flush.

"Don't I get to share?"

"Yes." Slowly he stripped the sheet downward. "In fact, you're a major part of this snack."

He reached into the bowl and selected a ripe juicy red berry.

"Open wide," he said.

He popped a berry into her mouth, and when she bit into it the juice ran down her chin. Steve bent over her and carefully licked the juice away. Then slowly, ever so slowly, he began to nibble at the other end of the berry.

He smelled of sunshine and wind and sweet clover hay, and in the early-morning sun he looked like one of those magnificent bronze statues she'd seen at Native American museums.

"Delicious," he murmured when his lips touched hers.

She was too busy to reply, too busy savoring the touch of his lips and tongue, too busy watching the way his eyes darkened as his passion rose, too busy enjoying the instant fire that swept through her.

As the kiss deepened he pressed her back against the covers. When they both had to come up for air, he looked into her eyes.

"I think I'll have another," he said.

"I hope it's as good as the first one."

"It will be better. I promise."

He stripped quickly, then reached toward the nightstand, and suddenly he was bending over her, a naked noble savage with a lethal-looking knife in his hand. With swift sure movements he sliced six berries, then carefully arranged them on her skin—two at the base of her neck, two on her nipples and two on her belly. Then he stood back to view his handiwork.

"A banquet fit for a savage," he said.

Delicious shivers shook her, and everywhere the berries touched, her skin was sensitized.

"Are you savage?" she whispered.

"Completely wild. On the rampage and looking for total surrender."

She opened her arms to him. "I surrender."

He bent over her and began to devour the berries, bit by sensuous bit. The berries were cold and juicy, his tongue and mouth hot. He bit into the fruit, letting the juice run in random patterns over her body, then slowly he licked the trail of juice.

Rocked by powerful sensations, she cried out, over and over, begging him for more.

Immersed in eroticism, drenched with passion, drowning in pleasure, screaming for completion, she reached for him, and he slid home.

The explosion shook her to the core, and she clung to him, limp and sated.

Still surrounded by her, he smiled down at her. "Did you enjoy your breakfast in bed?"

"Mmm." It was all she was capable of saying.

"Good. That was only the appetizer."

She'd thought she was spent, but when he began a deep slow thrusting, she discovered another dimension of her desire.

"You've made me insatiable," she murmured into the side of his neck.

His chuckle was as sexy as the rest of him.

"Good."

He took her on a meandering journey that lasted the rest of the morning, and when they fell against each other, drenched and complete, Steve brushed her damp hair off her forehead.

"I think I'll hold you captive in my bed," he said.

"There's nowhere else I'd rather be," she said, meaning it with all her heart.

Chapter Ten

She felt absolutely decadent, not getting up until two in the afternoon. Wrapped in a robe she'd found hanging on a hook in the bathroom, her hair wet and tied back with a ribbon, she found Steve in the kitchen downstairs.

"Do you ride?" he asked.

She blushed. "You should know."

His grin was wicked and knowing. "Horses?"

"Yes. But not without a western saddle."

"I want to show you the ranch this afternoon. We'll pack a picnic."

"Something smells good."

"Southern fried chicken. I thought it would make you feel right at home." He kissed her on the tip of the nose. "Grab some paper towels and help me with this."

They packed chicken piping hot from the pan, potato salad she made from her grandmother's recipe and a large thermos of hot coffee.

"This time of year nights get cold in high-desert country," he explained.

"What will I wear?" She looked down at her towel. "I can't go looking like this."

"While you were abed this morning, I had your camper delivered. I'll get your things. Did you bring a good warm jacket?"

"A couple of cotton sweaters."

"They won't do. We'll take one of my fleece jackets for you."

For somebody who had set out to prove she could take care of herself, Angel was feeling awfully content taking orders from Steve. Not orders, really, she told herself. Directions. After all, she was a guest on his ranch.

Steve felt as if he had stumbled into paradise. *Careful,* he kept telling himself. When something seems too good to be true, it generally is.

He watched Angel closely as they walked to the barn, studying her reaction to her surroundings. This ranch was his haven. A woman who didn't love it couldn't possibly be a part of his life.

The same was true of Lucas. If it came to a choice between a woman and his best friend, Lucas would win hands down.

Steve owed his life to Lucas. After that phone call in Saudi, Steve had tried to drown himself in the bottle. Probably would have, if Lucas hadn't flown to D.C., picked him up out of the gutter and carried him back to Arizona.

They were passing Steve's favorite spot on the ranch. Suddenly Angel stopped and put her hand over her heart.

"This is so beautiful I feel like crying. What is that magnificent formation?"

"Eagle Rock. If you stand beside it long enough, you can

almost always see eagles.'' Steve tipped her face upward. ''Look on the pinnacle. See that mass? That's their aerie. And look, there's one of the eagles.''

As she watched tears glimmered in her lashes. Steve caught them on his fingertips, then drew her into his arms and held her for a long time, his chin resting on the top of silky hair.

Almost, he could believe in a future.

''I have something to tell you.'' Her voice was muffled against his chest.

''All right.''

She tipped her face up to his. ''I love you, Steve Thunderhorse.''

Too full to speak, he squeezed her so close he could feel her heart pounding against his. Then he took her hand and led her to the barn.

Lucas was underneath a tractor, the only part of him visible a pair of scruffed-up boots.

''Lucas, come out here. There's somebody I want you to meet.''

Steve had the advantage of staring straight down at Lucas when his friend first saw Angel. Lucas treated her to the blue-eyed stare that had made men tremble in their boots. Angel stood perfectly at ease for this blatant inspection.

Lucas was never one to hide his feelings, and his face split in a wondrous grin. Then he was on his feet, wrapping Angel in a bear hug.

''Welcome to Paradise.'' Angel blushed and Lucas laughed. ''That's the name of our ranch. Corny, huh?''

''No. I think it's lovely…and appropriate.''

Steve loved the roses that flagged her cheeks, loved the soft dewy look in her eyes, loved the way she reached for his hand.

Lucas roared with laughter once more, than clapped Steve on the shoulder.

"Are you two going riding?"

Angel's mouth curved into a secret smile as she turned toward Steve. He squeezed her hand.

"Yes."

"Be sure and take her to Sunset Rock. I don't guess I can count on you being back in time for supper."

"No."

Lucas winked at Angel. "He's a man of few words, our Steve."

"That makes us a good pair. I'm a woman of millions of words."

Lucas hugged her again. "You're my kind of gal, Angel. That is, if I were looking for one. Have a great time, you two."

Steve saddled the gentlest mare in his stables for Angel. Her name was Molly, but both he and Lucas called her Old Slowpoke. She hated going faster than a slow trot, nothing spooked her, and she knew every nook and cranny of the ranch. If Angel was to be safe on a horse by herself, Slowpoke was the one.

"Are you sure you want me to ride her?" Angel looked askance at her mount. "She looks a little tired to me."

"She's reliable."

Thankfully Angel didn't argue. Steve brought Shadow around, threw a blanket over his back, then together they rode back to the house for the rest of their gear. He rode slightly behind Angel.

There was nothing wrong with the way she sat in the saddle. Steady. Good grip on the reins. Satisfied that she knew what she was doing, he rode up beside her.

"First I'll show you the paddocks."

He could have predicted Angel's reaction. Everybody

who came to Paradise Ranch was impressed when they saw the paddocks. Horses of almost every breed cavorted and pranced there—Appaloosas, paints, sturdy Chickasaws. He and Lucas had the reputation of being the best breeders and trainers in the West.

"I've never seen so many beautiful animals," Angel said. "Is this what you do?"

"Yes. Lucas and I breed and train. The Wild West Show is merely something I do to keep a bit of my Sioux heritage alive."

"Have you always done this?"

Her question was innocent, but the impact on Steve was totally unexpected. Memories swamped him. The deadlines, the late-night sessions with nothing but a cup of coffee and a glowing green cursor, the thrill of capturing exactly the right shot for his stories, the sense of accomplishment every time he typed his byline. Thunderhorse.

He thought of the awards stuffed in the back of his closet, the accolades, the readers who loved him and the ones who hated him. Success. But at what price?

Angel was waiting for his answer, looking at him in that quiet way of hers.

"No," he said. "I didn't always do this."

"What did you do before?"

It was a natural progression, one he was not prepared to take.

"Nothing of significance."

It was true. In the end everything he'd strived for, everything he'd achieved was meaningless. Success, without someone he loved to share it, was empty.

Lucas had told him it took courage to chuck it all and settle for a quiet life. Steve didn't know. Sometimes he thought of himself as a coward, hidden away in a remote ranch, never letting anything get close enough to mar his peace, never allowing anyone to breach his barriers.

And yet, here was Angel. Had she found his chinks, or had he been ready to allow someone inside?

He didn't know that, either. All he knew was that for the moment she was as necessary to him as breathing.

"Are you ready, Angel? We have lots of territory to cover before dark."

As it turned out, they didn't cover much territory on the ranch; they were too busy exploring the terrain of the heart.

High above the ranch house, Steve spread his blanket at the top of the sandstone bluff called Sunset Rock, where they watched the sun put on a spectacular evening show. Then they devoured fried chicken and each other.

"I love you, Steve," she said, and he wondered if miracles were possible. He wondered if the past could be wiped out so easily, with one blond-haired blue-eyed Angel.

The next morning Steve woke her with a kiss. Sleepy-eyed, she squinted up at him. He was already dressed and the sun was streaming through the windows.

"Morning, sleepyhead."

"What time is it?"

"Ten."

"Lolling in bed is getting to be a habit with me."

"You don't hear me complaining, do you?" He brushed her hair back and kissed one bare shoulder. "Mmm, delicious. Wish I had time for more."

Disappointment washed through her. "You don't?"

"There's a big horse sale down in Phoenix. Lucas and I will be taking six of the two-year-olds."

It was on the tip of her tongue to say, "Can I go?" but he was already dressed and obviously in a hurry. Besides she fancied a leisurely bath where she could soak neck-deep in bubbles and remember every searing detail of last night, starting with the lovemaking on Sunset Rock and ending with the erotic session they'd had in the hallway, all the way up the staircase and finally on the Oriental rug beside the bed.

She barely remembered Steve lifting her onto the bed and tucking her under the covers.

Smiling, she cupped his face and gave him a soft kiss.

"Have fun."

"You, too. I think you have everything you need here at the house. If not, ask Wayne. He's out at the stables if you need anything. He has strict orders to take care of you."

She kissed him again. "I'll be waiting for you."

"Good." He ruffled her hair. "Stay out of trouble."

She grinned impishly at him. "Ha. That'll be the day."

He turned at the door for one last look. She blew him a kiss, then padded barefoot to the bathroom for the soak she'd promised herself.

Afterward, she called Kaki. When she traveled their arrangement was that Angel would always let her assistant know where she could be reached in case of emergency.

"How's everything at home, Kaki?"

"Great. We heard a terrific lecture on the vanishing mountain gorilla at the university last night."

"We?"

"Your dad. You know how he loves that place. He'd go back in a heartbeat if he could. They lost a great teacher when he retired."

"Yes, they did."

Angel could picture it. Kaki all prim and proper with the man she was fond of calling "the font of information" sitting beside her, not only bringing the lecture alive but Kaki, too, telling her she looked pretty in pink or she should wear her hair down more often.

"How is he?"

"Fit as a fiddle. He's out in the garden now, gathering the last of the fall tomatoes. You want me to call him?"

"No, I just wanted to leave you this number."

As usual Kaki asked no questions. That way, Angel kept her privacy and her sense of independence while at the same time maintaining contact with the ones she loved.

Next she called Jenny. Her dearest friend. The person she most wanted to share her joy.

"You'll never guess where I am."

"Don't tell me, let me guess."

"That's what I said. Guess."

Jenny called this their who's-on-first routine. Both of them laughed, then Angel told her about Thunderhorse.

"I'm in love with him, Jenny."

"I see."

"*I see.* What kind of response is that? I've just told you that I've found the man I want to spend the rest of my life with, and all you can say is *I see* in a tone of voice that would chill Eskimos."

"What I didn't hear you say is that he loves you and has promised you everything your heart desires, including a moon made of green cheese. Has he said that?" Angel was silent. "I thought so. Furthermore, what are you doing on that godforsaken ranch besides you-know-what?"

"That's not fair."

"Honey, I'm not trying to be fair. I'm being brutally honest. From what I hear, you've described Texas all over again."

"Steve is not Dan, and this is not Texas. I'm not a prisoner here. I can do anything I want.'' Silence from Jenny's end. ''Have you been talking to Britt?''

''He did mention that he drove by that Wild West Show.'' Angel was too furious to comment. ''He said it looked like some fleabag operation.''

Angel gripped the receiver so hard her knuckles turned white.

''Just what do you know about this man, anyhow?''

''Enough, Jenny. I know enough.''

''All right, all right. I won't say any more about La La Land. Just remember the way home, Angel. And, honey, call me if you need me. Anytime day or night. Mother Jenny never sleeps.''

Angel was so mad she thought she might never call Jenny again. Didn't anybody trust her?

She wandered through the house, lingering in a small sun-lit room that faced the paddocks. She could work here. The space was friendly, open to the light. The kind of place that would welcome her muse.

She would sit right there beside the French doors so she would have a view of the trees, the lush pastures, the horses.

As she wandered back to the kitchen, Jenny's words haunted her. *Texas all over again.*

That was ridiculous. She was not a prisoner in Paradise. *You're my love slave.* Dan's words came to her unbidden, and she ran all the way to the stables to outrace them. When she arrived she was so out of breath she couldn't speak.

Wayne must have thought she was a crazy woman.

''Hi,'' he said. ''I'm Wayne.''

It took her a full minute before she could reply.

''I thought I'd go riding,'' she finally said.

''The boss thought you might. I'll saddle Slowpoke.''

Still mad about her phone call to Jenny, Angel rebelled.

"Not Slowpoke. Something with enough spunk to go more than five miles an hour."

Wayne laughed. "I don't know. Thunderhorse was very specific about the horse you were to ride."

"I'll take full responsibility."

Wayne scratched his head. "He's not going to like this."

"Look, I don't want to cause trouble. All I want is a decent mount and a good ride."

"All right. He did say you're a good horsewoman."

"He said that?"

Wayne was busy saddling a beautiful paint. "He did, and he's not one to pass out idle compliments."

Angel was as pleased as if she'd won a riding award.

Somewhat mellowed, she said, "Thank you, Wayne. I don't mean to be a pain."

"No. Lucas says you're a very fine lady."

Angel heard Jenny's voice saying, *What do you know about him?* Wayne could turn out to be a font of information if she asked the right questions. Not that she wanted to pry, and certainly not that she would ever go behind Steve's back and acquire information about him.

If she wanted to know something about Steve, she'd ask him. It was up to him to impart private information, in his own time, in his own way.

In a relationship that was called trust.

"Tell me about Lucas," she said. "Does he live at the house, too?"

"Gray Wolf?" Wayne laughed as if she'd made a huge joke. "No, ma'am. Thunderhorse built that house. You couldn't get Lucas to live in anything resembling a real house if your life depended on it."

"He doesn't live in a house?"

"Not exactly. He says a man should never have more

possessions than he can carry on his back, says anything with more space than a man can turn around in is too much. Winters he'll put his belongings in the bunkhouse, but mostly you'll see Gray Wolf in a bedroll sleeping under the stars.''

Wayne turned to Angel, smiling now, more at ease. ''Your mount's ready, ma'am. Her name is Stargazer, and she's as reliable as they come. Give her a little spin around the yard so the two of you can get acquainted.''

Angel didn't balk at that idea. No use earning the reputation of being difficult. She trotted the filly around the yard, and when she returned to the stables, Wayne, his hat pulled low over his eyes, was up on a beautiful black.

''Where to, ma'am?''

''You can call me Angel, and I'm just going up to Sunset Rock and back. By myself.'' At his look of alarm she added, ''I know the way.''

''I can't let you do that, ma'am. Thunderhorse would skin me alive.''

''There's no use arguing, Wayne. I'm going alone. You tell Thunderhorse if he's planning to skin anybody alive, it has to be me.''

''Ma'am—''

''Don't worry, Wayne, I'll be back before he gets home. And I plan to tell him what I did.''

She could see he was not convinced, so she tried another tack.

''I know you have work to do, and Sunset Rock is not more than a twenty-minute ride. Past the paddocks, left toward Deadman's Draw, then south along Thunder Creek. Right?''

Somewhat mollified, Wayne nodded. Angel's conscience twinged her only a moment, and then she was racing toward the paddocks on the powerful paint, the wind in her hair and freedom in her heart.

It was a glorious day, and when Steve got home, it was going to be an even more glorious evening.

The past could go take a hike, and tomorrow was soon enough to think about the future.

Chapter Eleven

The din inside the diner was deafening. Excitement ran high. Buyers and sellers, some elated over the day's deals, some disappointed, crowded the booths, wolfing down meat loaf and rehashing every detail of every sale.

Obviously in a hurry to get home, Steve concentrated on his food, but Lucas was too keyed up to eat. The annual horse sale in Phoenix was one of the country's best, and he loved every minute of it, the parade of excellent horseflesh, the high-stakes bidding, the behind-the-scenes dickering.

He glanced around the diner at the crowd—the waitress bent over to take an order, showing just the right amount of very fine leg, the old geezer with a wad of tobacco stuffed in his jaw and the buzzard feather in his hat, the dude rancher reading and drinking coffee at the same time.

Suddenly the headline caught Lucas's eye: ANGEL MERCER GOES SLUMMING. And underneath the headline was a picture of Thunderhorse carrying Angel out of Montezuma Mama's.

"I'll be back in a minute," he said, but Steve merely grunted and nodded.

The newsstand outside the diner carried papers from Phoenix, Tucson and Flagstaff. And Angel Mercer had made the front page of them all.

Lucas put his quarters into the slots and pulled out the papers. THE WRITER AND THE BROKEN-DOWN TRICK RIDER, shouted the Phoenix headline. ANGEL GOES SLUMMING, screamed the Tucson paper. It was the Flagstaff paper that really set Lucas's blood to boiling. ANGEL OF MERCY? the headline said, and beneath the picture the caption AN ALCOHOLIC'S LAST CHANCE?

Lucas scanned the articles. It was all there, every sleazy ugly detail of Steve Thunderhorse's past, including vitriolic quotes from his ex-wife, Emily. "What can you expect of a man who left his own wife to rot?" she'd told the reporter from Phoenix. "Of course he's resorted to gold digging. It takes lots of money to support an alcohol habit like his."

"It's a damned good thing you're in D.C., Emily, or I'd wring your pretty neck," Lucas muttered.

The reporters had done their background work well. The only thing they'd left out was the good stuff, the awards Thunderhorse had won, the prestige and respect he'd earned as a photojournalist, the fine journalistic work he'd done. Nor did any of them bother to mention that Thunderhorse had not had a drink in eight years, that he was, in fact, a successful and quite wealthy horse breeder and trainer.

Lucas filled the slots with money and bought every paper on the rack, then carried them to the men's room and trashed them. He knew he was only postponing the inevitable, but there was no use in ruining Steve's day.

Not when he had Angel waiting at home for him.

* * *

Angel was lost. It didn't take a Philadelphia lawyer to figure that out.

She'd had no trouble at all finding the place, then it was so peaceful on the rock she'd let time slip away. She guessed she'd waited too long to head home.

Everything looked different with the shadows on them.

Panic streaked through her. She'd been riding an hour, long past the time she should have been back at the ranch house. She'd heard about people getting lost in places like this. Sometimes they were never found.

Of course, Steve would come looking for her. Mad as a hornet. And poor Wayne. She hated to think about the wrath he would face.

Angel drew Stargazer to a halt, then dismounted and rubbed her aching backside. She wasn't used to sitting on a hard rock all afternoon. Nor was she accustomed to hours in the saddle.

"Get used to it, girl," she said, giving herself a pep talk. "If you're going to be living on a ranch with a full-blood Sioux, you'd better learn how to handle situations like this."

Somewhere in the distance something howled. A wolf? A wild dog?

She was going to be ripped to pieces. They'd never find a thing of her except a bit of hair and a few bones.

"Stop it."

Angel took several deep breaths. She had gotten herself into this mess, and she was going to get herself out. Period. End of discussion.

Slowly she mounted her horse, then she sat very still, looking around, taking stock.

There, in the distance? Wasn't that a copse of trees, and didn't trees grow beside water? If she could find Thunder

Creek, she could find home.

Angel headed in the direction of the trees.

"She's where?"

Steve's voice was deceptively calm. Wayne was scared to death. That much was obvious. Not of what Thunderhorse would do. Everybody knew he was not named Thunder for nothing, a lot of loud noise that generally blew over with the first good rain. It was fear for Angel that had Wayne twisted in knots.

Steve was so scared he could hardly breathe. Failure to keep watch over someone you loved was fatal.

Lucas put his hand on Steve's shoulder, a silent gesture of understanding.

"She can't be far, Steve. We'll find her."

Steve looked at the sky. There was half an hour of light left, maybe less. And not very good light at that. Evening was always filled with shadows, and for a woman alone, it was also filled with danger.

"Everybody saddle up," he said, surprised at how he could sound so calm when his heart was ripped in two. "Wayne, you go toward the canyons, Lucas you take the west range, and I'll head toward Sunset Rock."

Wayne had already saddled his horse in preparation for the search he knew was inevitable. He was already on the way while Lucas and Steve threw blankets over their mounts.

"Slowpoke would have had her home by now," Steve said. "She never misses her evening feed."

"Angel can be very persuasive," Lucas said.

How well Steve knew.

"Don't blame Wayne."

"I don't blame Wayne. I blame myself."

Lucas sprang onto his black stallion, then treated Steve with one of his deadly blue-eyed stares.

"That was nine years ago, Steve. It's over."

They rode in opposite directions, both going as fast as they dared in the evening gloom.

Angel was proud of herself. The trees had indeed meant water, and by looking at the pattern of shadows she'd been able to follow the creek in the correct direction.

"Who says I can't take care of myself? Right, Stargazer?"

Deadman's Draw was up ahead. She'd just spotted it when Thunderhorse came galloping into view.

"Angel!" he yelled.

Before she knew what was happening he'd swooped down on her and scooped her off her horse and onto his, all done at full gallop. He had her in a grip so tight she could barely breathe.

"Well," she said, when he drew Shadow to a halt. "I guess you're not a trick rider for nothing."

"I don't know whether to kiss you or kill you."

"Kiss me first."

And he did. It was a fierce possessive kiss that took her breath away. The kiss lasted so long she got vertigo from lack of oxygen. Not that she wanted to complain. Not one little bit.

When he released her she said, "Do that again."

Instead, he said, "Why did you leave the ranch by yourself?"

"You act as if I've committed a federal crime."

"I specifically told Wayne to go with you if you decided to take a ride."

"It was my fault, not Wayne's."

"Still, he defied my orders."

Angel was beginning to get mad. "Is that what this is about? Your orders?"

"No, this is about your safety. You don't know this ranch, nor even this country, Angel. It wasn't wise to go off by yourself."

He had a point, but she wasn't about to admit it.

"I am perfectly safe. In fact, I was on my way home when you came barreling out of nowhere and jerked me off my horse. Put me back on Stargazer. I'm going back to the ranch the same way I came—under my own power."

"You're going back with me."

Not only did he tighten his hold, but he caught Stargazer's reins and led her along beside them.

She shoved against his chest. "Put me down. I don't need you to rescue me."

"I'll put you down when we get home. Until then, sit still. You're spooking the horses."

She'd meant to huff and puff some more, but being in his arms felt too good. She'd save arguments till later. For now she was going to enjoy the ride.

When they reached the porch, he swung her down. "Wait right here."

"Why?"

"I've got to call back the search party. Don't you move a muscle."

The search party? Now she did feel bad. Not only that, she was embarrassed. Poor Wayne and Lucas. Tomorrow she would apologize.

The sound of a gong echoed across the ranch. Morose, Angel sat on the porch waiting for Steve. It was forever before he returned.

When he did he sat beside her on the porch steps and slid his arm around her.

"Sorry to be so long, Angel. I had to take care of the horses."

"I know." The tears that were clogged in her throat welled up in her eyes, much to her horror.

Steve's touch was tender as he wiped them away. "Don't cry, Angel," he whispered, drawing her close. "Everything's going to be all right."

Then he picked her up and carried her inside. It was only when they reached the bedroom that she thought of his choice of words. *Going to be all right?* Why hadn't he said, Everything *is* all right?

She didn't have time to ponder the question, for he was bending over her, unbuttoning her blouse. His mouth closed over her breast and she forgot everything except Thunderhorse and the exquisite pleasure that only he knew how to give.

Arching her back, she cupped her breasts and offered them up to him. Moaning, he drew her nipples deep into his mouth, first one, then the other. His ravenous suckling drove her wild. Weaving her hands into his hair, she pulled him so close she could feel his heart pounding against hers.

"I can't get enough of this," he murmured.

"I don't want you to."

She felt like a bowstring, her body so taut it fairly hummed. His tongue was hot and demanding, moving over her, ever downward, exploring territory he'd already charted and then some.

Tension built until the mere act of joining felt like release. *This,* she thought, *this is everything.*

Caught up in a primal dance both sweet and savage, they loved each other until the moon was on its descent. Slick and sated, she lay in his arms with her fingers buried in his chest hair.

"You are unbelievable," she whispered.

"It's us. Together."

She tried to recapture the feeling that what they had just

shared was everything, and yet she knew it was not true. The physical aspect of love was extremely important, but there were other aspects that had to be acknowledged.

"Steve, we need to talk."

He brushed her damp hair away from her forehead, then kissed her tenderly.

"Tomorrow, Angel. We'll talk tomorrow."

She might have protested had she not felt so content. In the wee hours of the morning, he awakened her with a bowl of strawberries in his hand and they took another erotic journey to fulfillment.

Was that the phone? It rang again.

"Steve?" Still groggy, she reached to his side of the bed. It was empty.

Pushing back the tangled covers, Angel sat up. Through the persistent ringing of the phone came the sound of water running. Steve must be taking a shower.

She picked up the receiver. "Paradise Ranch," she said.

"Angel?" It was Jenny.

"How did you get this number?"

"Don't hang up. It's an emergency."

"Dad?"

"No. Turn on the TV."

"What can possibly be so important—"

"Don't argue. Just do it. Now!"

"Which channel?"

"It doesn't matter. It's on all of them."

Angel found the remote control and started flipping through the channels. Suddenly she froze. There was a blowup of Thunderhorse carrying her from the restaurant. The voice-over was done by a female apparently taking great relish in revealing the juicy details of the relationship.

"Angel Mercer, the writer famous for her detective novels starring the saucy angel Muriel has found a new source for inspiration—Steve Thunderhorse, a man who spends his time these days riding a trick horse in a Wild West Show.''

Angel groaned. ''Angel?'' Jenny's voice squawked at her from the receiver she'd laid in her lap. ''Did you get it?''

''Yes.''

''We'll talk later.''

Angel turned her attention back to the television.

''Once a Pulitzer prize–winning journalist, Thunderhorse dropped from sight nine years ago after the brutal murder of his daughter, Sunny.''

Angel's blood drained from her face, and she pressed her hand over her heart to hold back the hurt. To lose a child had to be the most devastating blow life could deal.

The commentator continued, ''Thunderhorse could not be reached for comment about his liaison with Angel Mercer, but we did interview his ex-wife, Emily.''

Emily was a tall brunette who must have been pretty at one time. Lines of discontent bracketed her mouth, and the puffiness under her eyes was evidence of sleepless nights. And perhaps more.

''Emily, will you comment on your ex-husband's liaison with Angel Mercer?''

''He married me for my money, and now he's after hers. It takes money to be an alcoholic.''

''Emily, is it true that both you and Steve Thunderhorse received treatment at Richmond's Drug and Alcohol Rehabilitation Clinic?''

''Yes.'' Emily glared at the camera. ''What would you do if somebody murdered your child and your husband abandoned you?''

The hairs on the back of Angel's neck stood on end, and slowly she turned her head toward the bathroom. Steve was standing in the doorway, a towel knotted at his waist, his wet feet dripping on the rug.

"Steve." She made a move toward him, but the look on his face stopped her.

"Have you heard enough?"

"Oh…" Her heart was hurting so badly she couldn't speak. She picked up the remote control and flicked off the television.

Mercifully the screen went blank. The silence in the room was deafening. Steve stood rigid in the doorway and she sat rigid on the bed. The Grand Canyon separated them, the Pacific Ocean, Mount Everest.

And she could think of nothing that would span the chasm. She licked her dry lips.

"How…how long have you been standing there?"

"Long enough."

Steve threw his towel into the bathroom, then strode to the dresser and began to jerk on his clothes. A button popped off his shirt and rolled across the floor.

Angel stared at the button until it blurred. Blinking back tears, she left the bed and put her hand on Steve's arm. He went still as a rock, a statue, a block of ice.

"It's was horrible, Steve. Everything they said."

"Yes. It was horrible."

His voice sent shivers along her spine, and she wrapped her arms around herself as if warding off a chill.

"That didn't come out right.… I don't know what to say." She glanced at him. His eyes were terrible, black ice, frozen in the mask of his face.

"What part of it didn't you understand, Angel? The part about my alcoholism? The part about me abandoning my wife? The part about me being a broken-down trick rider?"

"Oh, Steve." She wrapped her arms around him. It was

like embracing a hardwood tree. "None of that's true. I know it's not."

He disentangled himself. With one hand gripping her wrists, he pried open her fingers.

"Is that why your hands are balled into fists? Is that why you've cut your palms with your fingernails? Because you don't believe a word you've heard?"

"It's because I hurt for you, Steve. For your loss, for Sun—"

His voice cut through her knifelike. "Don't say it. Don't say her name."

He held her wrists so tightly her skin was turning the blanched white of marble. There must be a thousand things to say, but she could think of only one.

"I'm so sorry, Steve," she whispered. "I'm so sorry."

He was staring at a point just beyond her, not the picture on the wall, not the cottonwood tree visible through the window, not the red rooftop of the stables, but of a distant time, a distant place where an unspeakable tragedy had forever altered the course of his life.

No matter how hard she tried, Angel could never go there. She could never know the man he once was, never feel his gut-wrenching pain, never share his heartrending sorrow. Compassion carried her only so far. Empathy gave her only a fraction of the turmoil.

"I know that nothing I can say will alleviate your pain, but I will gladly share it with you when you want to talk…if you want to talk."

His frozen expression remained unchanged, but his grip on her wrists loosened.

"Whatever happened, whatever happens, I love you, Steve."

She caught back a sob. She would *not* cry, not now, not when he needed her to be strong.

"I love you." She leaned down and kissed the inside of his wrist.

Awareness crept back to him. It showed in the slackening of his grip, the color bathing his face, the twin points of light that came into his eyes.

Hope leaped through her. Everything was going to be all right.

Steve lifted her hands, palms up, to his mouth. There was tenderness in the way he kissed them. And sadness. Such sadness that her heart wept.

His face became shuttered again, and when he released her, a cold fear gripped Angel.

"You can stay here as long as you like," he said.

"What do you mean? Where are you going?"

"I'm going to bring a herd of horses in from the north range. Winter's coming soon."

Angel shivered. Winter was already here. A bitter winter of the heart.

"Don't go, Steve. Not like this."

"There's nothing else to say, Angel."

"There's a world of things to say. I love you, Steve."

He studied her as if he was committing her to memory. Finally he spoke.

"So did Sunny—and I killed her."

Paralyzed by shock and fear, she watched him walk away from her. In three strides he was across the room. He passed the bed without a glance, the bed where only hours earlier they had made love to the point of exhaustion and bliss. He never even glanced at the bowl of leftover berries, never looked once at the berry stains on the sheets.

Her dreams were turning to vapor, and she was powerless to change things. He was already at the door when she called after him.

"Wait...."

For a moment he hesitated, and she thought he would turn and come back to her.

"Steve, please," she whispered.

She wouldn't go to him, wouldn't hang on like a beggar. He had to come back to her.

"Don't go. Not like this."

He stood very still in the doorway, and with every second that passed, her hopes lifted. Then, without warning, his back stiffened and he left.

His footsteps, resolute and determined, resounded down the hallway and echoed on the staircase. Angel stood in the middle of the bedroom not moving, barely breathing. Even after the front door slammed, she stood perfectly still, waiting for him to return, unwilling to believe that he would actually leave her.

Time was suspended. Every detail of the room became magnified—Steve's button on the floor, the half-empty bowl of strawberries, the bed.

Oh, God. The bed. Pain slashed through Angel, and she wrapped her arms around herself to contain it.

In the distance she heard the pounding of hooves. She raced to the window and saw the white stallion and his rider thunder by.

"Steve."

Did she call his name? Whisper it? Think it?

Surely he heard. Surely he wouldn't leave her without a backward glance.

He rode past Eagle Rock, past the house, past the paddocks without a glance. Angel's fingernails bit so deeply into her palms she brought blood.

Just past the paddocks the stallion came to a halt, and Steve gazed toward the house.

"Come back," she whispered. "Please come back."

For a moment she thought he would. He leaned forward,

pointing the stallion's head toward home. Angel pressed her hand over her heart, waiting.

Suddenly the stallion wheeled, then galloped out of sight. Steve was gone, and Angel's world would never be the same.

Chapter Twelve

Angel found Lucas in the barn.

After she'd picked herself up and put herself back together again with a good hot soak in the tub, she'd dressed, then gone in search of Steve Thunderhorse's best friend.

He was sitting on a bale of hay just inside the wide barn aisle, smoking a pipe. She didn't try to hide her relief.

"I'm so glad to see you," she said.

"I thought you'd want to talk to me. I started to come to the house, then I decided to wait for you out here." He took a deep draw on his pipe. "Have a seat."

He indicated the bale of hay next to his. Angel sat down, her hands twisted together like pretzels, her back rigid, her neck stiff. Now that she was here, she didn't quite know how to begin.

"Take some deep breaths, Angel." Lucas puffed on his pipe. "There's something peaceful about being in a barn if you let yourself be still long enough to appreciate it."

His quiet reassurance was balm to her soul. Angel gulped back the sobs that were still caught in her throat, then closed her eyes and let herself smell the hay, listen to the soft snorting of horses and cooing of pigeons, feel the warmth of the sun coming through the open barn doors.

If she sat there long enough, would Steve come back? Would he say, "I'm sorry, Angel, let's start all over"? Would he say, "I want to tell you what happened"?

"I suppose you want to know about Steve."

Angel swallowed the lump in her throat. "I don't want you to think I've come out here to sneak around behind his back or to ask you to break confidences."

"No. I'm a good judge of people. That wouldn't be your way." Lucas tamped out his pipe. "Nine years ago Steve was the best war correspondent in the country. He'd won more awards than any photojournalist his age had a right to expect, including a Pulitzer."

Lucas studied her quietly. "I guess you heard that already."

"Yes. This morning...on TV."

"What you won't hear is that he was well respected and well loved. He was a good husband, a wonderful father and an altogether decent human being."

"I knew that. In here." Angel put her hand over her heart.

"Steve Thunderhorse is one of the finest people I know. We grew up together, went to school together. The Thunderhorses were wealthy people, some said snobbish. His father was a nuclear physicist and his mother a concert pianist." Lucas chuckled. "Steve didn't inherit her musical talent, though that doesn't keep him from trying."

A vision of Steve playing his guitar at the campground flashed into her mind, and Angel's heart contracted.

"I was an orphan, somebody kids like Steve rarely noticed. He not only noticed, he took my side in a schoolyard brawl when we were six. We've been friends ever since. There's nothing I wouldn't do for him, including trying to keep the woman he loves from turning against him.''

"He loves me?"

"Yes, he loves you."

"Has he told you so?"

"I didn't have to hear the words. Steve speaks with his heart."

"Then why did he leave me?" She thought of the way he had looked standing in the doorway while the television reporter spewed forth venom. Angry. Cold. And betrayed.

"He should have known I wouldn't believe those horrible things they were saying about him. Of all people, I understand how rumor and innuendo can pass for the truth."

"It had nothing to do with you, Angel. Steve left because he's afraid he'll fail you, just as he believes he failed his family nine years ago."

"Can you tell me what happened?"

"He was in Saudi Arabia, covering the conflict there. Emily and Sunny decided to go skating one day. Halfway to the rink, Sunny discovered she'd forgotten her skates. They turned around and went back to the house, and when they walked inside they interrupted a burglar. He panicked and raced out the back door, but not before throwing the VCR at them."

Chills ran through Angel. She knew what was coming next, and every atom in her body willed it not to be so. She wanted to turn back the clock and have the burglar make his escape while Emily called the police and Sunny retrieved her skates.

But she couldn't write happy endings for real life.

"The VCR hit Sunny in the temple," Lucas said. "She was dead by the time they got her to the hospital."

Silent tears rained down Angel's face. Lucas handed her a handkerchief.

"The death of their child almost destroyed both of them. They turned to the bottle for comfort. Steve kicked the habit. Emily didn't."

"They divorced?"

"Eventually. Emily filed after he came out here. It was just a formality. Their marriage ended the day Sunny died."

Angel sat quietly, absorbing the story. There were huge gaps of course, but it was fairly easy to fill in the missing pieces. Steve lost his child while he was in another part of the world doing his job, so he held himself responsible.

It explained a lot of things—why he'd wanted her to ride a horse that could barely move, why he'd insisted Wayne accompany her, why he was always so protective, as if she were made of glass.

It also explained his fear. His past was still haunting him. He'd pushed it aside long enough to have a brief idyll with her, but the minute the news media unearthed it, he'd run.

And he wasn't coming back. The truth settled in her heart like a stone.

Standing, Angel brushed the hay off her jeans. "Thank you, Lucas."

He squinted up at her. "What are you going to do?"

"I'm going home."

"I wish I could convince you to stay. I wish I could tell you that when Steve returns with the horses, he'll have had time to think everything through and realize that he wasn't the one who failed."

"It's not going to happen." The look on his face confirmed what she already knew: Lucas agreed. They both knew Steve Thunderhorse well.

Lucas unfolded his long legs and tucked his pipe into his pocket. "I'll help you load up."

"I appreciate that, Lucas."

It took them only an hour to get all her gear together, and during that time she came to understand how Lucas must have been a tremendous factor in Steve's recovery. He was one of those easygoing open-faced men you naturally trusted, the kind of man you felt you could tell anything to and he wouldn't lift an eyebrow.

He waited until he'd stowed the last of her luggage into her camper before he dropped his bombshell.

"I'll go over to the bunkhouse and get Wayne."

"Wayne?"

"Steve thought you might be leaving. He told Wayne to drive you home."

Angel felt like throwing something. "Wayne is *not* going to drive me home. I got here under my own power, and I'll leave the same way."

"I told Steve it wasn't going to work that way, but he's so blamed stubborn he didn't listen to a thing I said."

"He's not the only one who can be stubborn." She set her jaw like a bulldog's. She was through with having people tell her what to do.

"I've seen that look before, and when I do, I know better than to mess with it." Lucas leaned in the doorway as she climbed into her camper. "There are some winding back roads between here and the highway. At least let me lead you out."

He was right. She remembered the roads. She would be foolish to refuse his offer.

"All right," she said. "And, Lucas, thanks for everything."

"You bet."

She was glad he didn't spew empty words at her. One of the most destructive emotions in the world was false hope.

Lucas returned, and for the next forty-five minutes she

concentrated solely on keeping up with his motorcycle. Suited and helmeted, he looked like a Martian. The illusion added to her surreal feeling.

She was in the midst of one of her own plots, and when she wrote ''The End,'' she would walk away from her computer and back into her real life. She was in the midst of a movie, and when the final credits rolled, she would walk outside into the sunshine and find Steve Thunderhorse waiting for her, sitting atop his white stallion.

The highway loomed ahead. Lucas slowed his bike, then pulled over to the side.

She was not in the midst of a fantasy; she was in the midst of reality.

''I won't think about the future,'' she told herself. One day at a time, her grandmother used to say. The old adage had a certain amount of wisdom. And comfort.

Angel amended it to one *moment* at a time. And for this moment she pasted a brave smile on her face, then lifted her hand in farewell to Lucas.

He gave her a thumbs-up when she drove by. In her rearview mirror she saw him turn the bike and head back home.

Home. For a beautiful few days she'd thought home was Paradise Ranch. Now she faced the stark truth: Home was a faraway place that she would reach after a long journey. Alone.

Angel set her face eastward, toward the sun.

Chapter Thirteen

A wild stallion had come into the herd. He was a beauty, powerfully built, deep black, his long mane and tail floating behind him like the flags of some exotic foreign country.

Steve called him Satan. And not without reason. He had one of the quickest meanest tempers Steve had ever seen in a horse. At the slightest provocation he would snort and paw the ground, then rear into the air screaming his challenge, his forelegs beating the air and anything else that came within range.

Any other time Steve would have cut him out of the herd, then started back to the ranch. But not this time. This time he needed the distraction. He needed the challenge. He needed the adrenaline rush that was part fear, part exultation.

Anything to take his mind off Angel.

Where was she now? Still at the ranch? Was she curled under the covers waiting for him, soft and sweet and warm?

If he hurried he might still have time to get back to her. He might still have time to hold her in his arms. He might still have time to kiss her, to love her.

Stop it.

If he continued to think about her, he would drive himself mad. Pressing his knees into Shadow's sides, he thundered through the canyons, driving himself, as well as his herd, toward protection.

If the signs were any indication, a long hard winter would soon settle over the land. And if it was as barren as the winter that had settled over his heart, Paradise Ranch was in for a rough time.

Angel made better time going home than she had coming. For one thing she was traveling roads that were at least vaguely familiar. For another, she wasn't stopping as much to sightsee. Her goal was to get back to Mississippi as fast as possible, back to the comfort of her dad and Kaki, back to the comfort of her porch swing and her flower garden, even back to the comfort of the glowing green cursor on her computer.

A story was being born, even as she drove. Muriel would fall in love. It happened. Even to angels.

Suddenly the roar of the waterfall came to her, and Steve was standing beside her saying, ''I wanted to give you the world.''

The road blurred so badly she had to pull off at the nearest gas station so she could cry herself out. How many tears could a heartbroken woman shed?

Mad at herself, mad at him, Angel pulled out a soggy handkerchief and mopped her tears. The face peering back at her from the mirror was blotched and red. Not her face at all.

''This will not do,'' she said. ''This will not do at all.''

She wasn't about to go home defeated and weepy. For one thing she didn't want to worry her dad. For another she didn't want to give Kaki and Jenny and Britt a chance to say I told you so.

Food, that was what she needed. She made sure her camper was properly parked, then went into the gas station to see if they had pimento-cheese sandwiches wrapped in plastic in those wretched coolers. Or at the very least, crackers with peanut butter. She needed protein. She needed fuel. She needed Steve.

Sobs bubbled up, but she choked them back. She had to stop crying or she would never be able to go home.

Where was she, anyway?

She looked for signs. One just south of the gas pumps said: Little Rock, 112 miles. She was already in Arkansas. She would cross the Mississippi River into Tennessee, then head south toward Mississippi.

Missing Texas altogether.

The storekeeper said they were out of pimento-cheese sandwiches. "But we got plenty a' ham, honey, and I'll zap it in the microwave for you."

Her name was May Belle, and when she said *I'll,* it came out *ah'll,* and Angel could feel her troubles melting away. As long as she had this—the welcome sound of the Southern drawl, the open friendliness of strangers, the signposts that led back home—she could survive.

"Would you please do that?" she said, and even though her smile was strained and she knew she must look like something from a late-night horror show, May Belle never let on. She just said, "Sure thang, honey. You jes set over there and rest yourself while I heat this thang up." She patted Angel's hand. "Even famous folks has to have a good cry ever now and then."

By the time Angel ate her sandwich, her courage was

inching up. She thanked May Belle once again for her hospitality, then headed to her camper. She was halfway in the door when she knew she wasn't going to head toward the Mississippi River.

She went back into the store and asked May Belle if there was a phone she could use.

"Over yonder by the toilets, sugah. Behind the 'tater chips."

Angel called home.

"Dad?"

"Angel!" It was wonderful to hear his voice. The way he said her name was heaven, full of soft surprise and happiness, drawn out as it was two words.

"Are you all right, sweetheart? I started to call you after that story broke, but decided it would be best to wait until you were ready to talk about it."

"I'm fine, Dad." An outright lie. The first she'd ever told her father. "I'm in Arkansas."

"You're on the way home, then?"

"Not yet. There's something I have to do first."

Carl Mercer was quick to pick up his daughter's train of thought. She'd once accused him of being clairvoyant, and he'd said that often people with strong connections of the heart have a telepathy that makes words redundant.

"You be careful down in Texas, you hear?"

"Thank you for understanding, Daddy. Thank you for not trying to talk me out of this."

"I wouldn't dream of it. This trip has been a long time in coming. It's something you've been needing to do for years."

"You never told me that."

"It wasn't my decision to make. It was yours. I knew you'd do it when the time was right."

"I'll be home in a few days, Daddy."

"You're a champ, sweetheart, and don't you forget it."

Angel got gas, then climbed back into the camper and headed south. Toward Texas.

They had torn down the shanty where she and Dan Calloway once lived. In its place was a park where children romped with happy abandon, their laughter lifting toward the sky like bright kites.

Angel parked the camper and walked to a park bench underneath a canopy of trees. Around the park houses had sprung up like mushrooms, houses complete with front porches and well-kept lawns. They overlooked shady streets where lampposts would glow after the sun went down, casting light on the sidewalks so children in the park could find their way home.

A woman pushing a chubby little boy in a stroller sat down on the other end of the bench.

"How long has this park been here?" Angel asked her.

"Five years."

Angel thought of all those wasted years she'd spent being afraid to come back to a place that no longer even existed. Not only was the ugly shanty gone, but in its place was something of beauty, a neighborhood where children could play and dream, children full of the promise of the future.

The little boy in the stroller started to cry, and his mother handed him a sugar cookie and a handful of raisins. Then she turned to Angel.

"Say, are you...? No, you couldn't be. You want a cookie?"

"Yes. Thank you."

Angel munched her cookie, then sat on the bench till the sun went down. One by one the children and their parents and assorted dogs left the park to return home.

Angel found a small motel out on Interstate 10 near the

gas station where she'd called home for help so many years ago. Tomorrow she would go there and face that dragon. Then she'd have only one more ghost to put to rest.

Dan Calloway. If she could find him.

Steve had never seen Lucas so mad. He stood at the fence, glaring into the paddock.

"What are you trying to do?" Lucas asked. "Kill yourself?"

"I thought you were in the north pasture."

"Obviously."

Lucas took his pipe out of his pocket and tamped in the tobacco in angry jerky motions. Steve walked over to join him, glad for the break. Beads of perspiration rolled down his face and onto his shirt, creating big wet patches.

In the corner of the paddock stood Satan, his body tense, muscles rippling, nostrils flared, black coat shining with sweat.

Lucas nodded in his direction. "You know how I feel about that stallion. He's a killer."

"He's one of the finest pieces of horseflesh I've seen in years."

"Nobody will ever break him. Not even you."

"It will take a little time and patience, that's all."

"He'll break you first, Steve. Is that what you want?"

There was no point in answering that question. Lucas had already made up his mind, and once he did that, there was no changing it. He and Steve were equally stubborn. It was a wonder they'd managed to be friends all these years, let alone partners.

"Shadow is getting old," Steve said. "Satan will be a good replacement."

"You need a white stallion for the show. Sitting Bull had a white stallion."

Steve let that slide, too. He might cancel everything his agent had booked and never do another Wild West Show. How could he bear to do the waltz without Angel?

He turned and headed back toward the stallion.

"You could go after her," Lucas said.

There was no such thing as reversing the past. Lucas, of all people, should know that.

"She loves you, you know," Lucas called.

Steve kept on walking.

The gas station hadn't changed much. They'd added a new pump and a new billboard out front. Other than that, everything was pretty much the same. Even the man who stood behind the cash register.

When Angel first stepped into the store, disguised, shivers ran down her spine. There was the candy rack with the Mars bars she'd told Dan she wanted. There was the telephone she'd used to call her dad. There was the toilet she'd hid in until Dan grew impatient waiting for her, then pounded on the door, shouting her name.

Public displays never bothered him. That was why Angel was certain nearly anybody who'd ever seen him would remember him.

The hair at the back of her neck prickled, and she found herself skirting the candy-bar rack.

"This won't do," she whispered.

Gathering her courage, she approached the rack, then made herself stand there long enough for the shivers to go away. Finally she selected her candy. A Mars bar. Dan used to buy them in six-packs and bring them home as gifts of contrition after he'd done some horrible thing. Once he'd kept her locked in the bathroom for two days because she'd told him no when he tried to claim his early-morning "privileges,'' as he called it. When he finally let her out, he'd handed her a single red rose and a box of Mars bars.

The sight of red roses still made her sick.

She adjusted her sunglasses, pulled her hat down low, then took the candy bar to the cash register to pay.

''Will that be all, miss?''

Would it? Hadn't she already seen enough without seeing Dan, too?

Her father's voice echoed through her mind. *You're a champ, Angel. And don't you forget it.* Then Steve stole into her heart. Steve had given her the world—and with it, courage.

''I was wondering…'' she said. ''Do you happen to remember a man named Dan Calloway?''

''Big guy with brown wavy hair and those perfect teeth that looked like he could pose for toothpaste commercials?''

Angel could still walk away. She could simply say, ''No, that's not the one,'' then walk out the door.

''Yes.'' Her voice was no more than a whisper. She cleared her throat. ''Yes,'' she said loudly, too loudly. ''That's the one.''

''He used to come in here all the time to buy Mars bars.''

Could she handle this? Angel made herself stand perfectly still.

''Yes, he did,'' she agreed. ''Do you happen to know where I can find him?''

''Reckon I do. He's at Lawndale. Been there about three years.''

''Lawndale? I don't recall a town by that name.''

''The cemetery. He keeled over next door while he was eating a mess of Jim's barbecued ribs. One minute he was eating and the next his heart quit, and he just fell face forward into his plate.''

Somehow it didn't seem appropriate to tell the man thank-you. Instead, Angel asked for directions to Lawndale, then she drove into town and bought a single red rose to place on Dan Calloway's grave.

Chapter Fourteen

Angel felt like the cowardly lion. But instead of going to Oz, she went to Texas to get her courage back. Careful to avoid the TV and newspapers, she stayed three days, not to see the sights but to prove to herself that the miracle wasn't a fluke.

Of course, some folks wouldn't call confronting your past and laying all your ghosts to rest a miracle, but Angel did. That was the way she was. She wrote about miracles in every book, and she believed in them, too. First, there had been the miracle of Steve, and then one in a gas station in Texas.

The woman who drove home to Mississippi was not the same woman who had left. Pieces of herself that had been missing for years were suddenly intact. When Angel got out of her camper, her feet made solid contact with the ground. There was confidence in her stride and a vaulting sense of freedom in her heart.

She was a woman made to wear boots. With her new red leather boots planted firmly on the front porch, she announced her arrival.

"Dad...Kaki. I'm home."

They burst through the door, her father first, and Angel was caught up in a flurry of hugs and kisses and joyful exclamations.

"I'm so glad you're back, sweetheart." Her dad leaned back to study her, then apparently satisfied by what he saw, he hugged her close again. "It's *good* to have you home."

He made no mention of Thunderhorse and the awful stories that had dominated the news. He'd never been one to intrude into her private affairs.

Nor had Kaki. "You look wonderful," she said.

"So do you." Angel meant it. There was something different about Kaki. Not the hair—it was still pulled into a tight little knot. The clothes were the same, and yet not entirely. She was wearing a suit, yellow linen, new from the looks of it, but somehow she still looked different. Maybe it was the cut of the suit, the shorter skirt, the almost casual line in the jacket. Or perhaps it was her blouse.

That was it. Kaki was wearing one of those crisp little white spandex tops with a single gold chain resting against her skin. And that was another thing. Kaki had a tan.

This surprised Angel. She had never considered her research assistant the outdoor type.

"Your color is good, Kaki. Have you been swimming?"

Kaki actually blushed. Another first.

"Not exactly." She fiddled with the chain around her neck. "I did go on a picnic or two while you were gone."

"Great."

Unlike her dad and Kaki, Angel was the nosy type, and she was dying to know more. But they were all still standing on the front porch, and Mr. Edwards across the street had come out onto his front porch to gawk, and besides, since they'd been polite enough not to dig into the private details of her life, she would return the favor.

For the time being, at least.

"If I'd known you were going to be home today, I'd have made some of your favorite tea," her dad said.

Angel was surprised again. In summers and well into fall, her dad always kept a pitcher of tea in the refrigerator. He was rummaging around in there now, and when he emerged he was smiling.

"How about a power drink?" Without waiting for confirmation he poured three glasses of an orange liquid.

Angel picked hers up to sniff. "What is it?"

"Carrots, tomatoes and a few other vegetables pulverized in the blender. Kaki put me on it."

Carl Mercer's eyes seemed brighter than when Angel had left. His color was better, too. Whatever he'd been doing agreed with him.

And was it Angel's imagination, or was there a certain spark in the smile he turned in Kaki's direction?

She was being foolish of course. Carl Mercer was always trying to make Kaki feel good about herself.

Just because Angel was attuned to sparks and secret smiles and significant glances didn't mean the whole world had fallen in love during her absence.

"I've always believed in taking care of your health," Kaki said.

Then to Angel's complete astonishment Kaki pulled off her jacket before she sat down. Her arms were very nice for a woman her age. Especially with that new tan.

Angel was going to tell Kaki so, but her dad beat her to it.

"You look especially lovely today, Kaki."

''Thank you.'' The smile she turned in his direction was positively radiant.

Kaki looked the way Angel had felt when she was with Steve, as if someone had set off sparklers in her heart. Could it be that Kaki had fallen in love?

Angel wasn't about to pursue that subject. Just thinking about love and all its tender pleasures made her weak with longing. The tears she thought she'd left behind threatened to spill over.

She took a big gulp of her drink, wishing it would actually do what her dad claimed. Angel needed to feel powerful—and she knew one surefire way to do it.

''Listen, you two, I don't mean to be a party pooper, but a really good story idea came to me while I was driving. I'm going to race into my office and get something on paper while my muse is still with me.''

She hadn't exactly told a lie. Her muse *was* with her, but once Angel was in her office she didn't race to her computer. Instead, she leaned against the closed door and cried. She cried for herself, she cried for Steve, she cried for what might have been.

And when there were no more tears left, she turned on her computer and typed: ANGEL IN LOVE—Synopsis.

As always, when she was writing time became meaningless. Her fingers fairly flew over the keyboard. She was startled when the tapping came on her door. Kaki stuck her head around the door frame.

''I don't mean to disturb you, but dinner's ready.''

''Dinner?'' Angel glanced at the clock. It was already seven. ''Good grief, Kaki, what are you still doing here?''

''I thought you might need me to do a few extra things, since this is your first night back and all.''

Kaki's jacket was still off and her hair was down. In fact, she looked decidedly mussed.

"You work too hard," Angel said. "Scat. Shoo. There's nothing pending that we can't take care of tomorrow."

"Actually, your dad invited me to stay for dinner. He made meat loaf. Your favorite."

"Great. Suddenly I'm starved." Angel shut down her computer, then linked arms with Kaki. "Dad's the sweetest man."

"You won't get any argument from me."

Was that another blush on Kaki's cheeks? What in the world was going on?

Nothing, she told herself an hour later. Absolutely nothing was going on except that Carl Mercer was being his usual generous self in making Angel's homecoming feel like a party for all of them.

"Anybody for a little after-dinner stroll?" he said.

"Not me," Angel said. "I'm bushed. If you don't mind, Dad, I think I'll take a raincheck."

"No problem at all, sweetheart." He was all smiles when he turned to Kaki. "Ready, Kaki?"

Angel was in the tub before it hit her what her dad had said. Not *Do you want to go, Kaki?* but *Ready, Kaki?* as if they'd been planning this stroll all along. Or as if they did this kind of thing every evening, like a couple who had been together long enough to have a routine and ways of communicating that didn't need words and private jokes.

"Good grief. Stop this."

Angel was disgusted with herself. Once she got her writer's mind going, she couldn't turn it off.

"Might as well join them and settle this once and for all."

She got out the tub, toweled herself off and put on fresh jeans. She was rummaging in her closet for a cotton sweater when she happened to glance out the window. A full moon illuminated the garden and the two figures on the garden path. Her dad and Kaki. In each other's arms. Kissing.

"It can't be."

Angel moved closer to the window, not spying, she told herself. Merely satisfying her curiosity.

"After all, this is my daddy we're talking about...and my research assistant."

It didn't take a Philadelphia lawyer to figure out what was going on beneath her window. Carl and Kaki were definitely locked in an embrace, and they were definitely kissing.

And not just a chaste kiss, either. Not even a hearty good-friend kiss. There was deep familiarity in the kiss. And passion. Honest-to-goodness fire that made Angel step back from the window feeling as guilty as if she'd walked into their bedroom.

Their bedroom? Was it possible? Her father and Kaki?

After all these years of hoping that her dad would let her mother go gently into the night, Angel found herself feeling left out and somewhat miffed, as if they had done something behind her back that she didn't quite approve of.

That was ridiculous of course. She considered her dad incapable of doing wrong, and she absolutely adored Kaki. As a person, as well as an employee. And there was about ten years' difference in their ages.

Her dad and Kaki. It was perfect.

Almost.

They had each other and she had nobody. She felt like an interloper in her own house, a third wheel, a nuisance, somebody whose mere presence spoiled what was otherwise a perfect setup for lovers.

Angel's heart felt wrenched. A week ago she'd been in the same position—a woman in love, securely ensconced in a house she and Steve had made their own. There wasn't a corner of that ranch house that didn't hold a special memory. The staircase, the shower, the Oriental rug in the library, the barn...

Angel clamped her hands over her ears as if that could hold her thoughts at bay. Moving as if demons were in hot pursuit, she jerked out a CD by Cher and put it in the player—BELIEVE.

Wrong choice. It was all about discovering whether there was life after love.

She turned it off and cried herself to sleep.

When the weather was nice, Angel and her father always had breakfast together in the backyard. It was a cherished ritual, one Angel looked forward to. It was also a good way to start the day, surrounded by nature and in the company of her wise and loving father.

Sometimes they talked while they ate, and sometimes they merely sat in companionable silence, appreciating the good food, reading the morning paper and listening to the sounds of nature, the mockingbirds quarreling over possession of the birdbath, the whirr of hummingbird wings, the sighing of wind in the trees.

This morning the paper was conspicuously absent.

"I have to talk to you, Angel. Got your ears on?"

He never began conversations that way unless the matter was serious. Angel shoved her plate aside. She wasn't hungry, anyway. She was too busy thinking of strawberries in a pottery bowl and the magnificent Sioux who had fed them to her.

"I'm listening, Dad."

"It's about..." He paused, cleared his throat and started again. "While you gone, I made a remarkable discovery."

"That you can't live without me?" she said, teasing him.

Smiling, he took her hand. "That's true. You are the joy

of my life, Angel. I don't know what I would have done these last three years if it hadn't been for you."

His choice of words alerted her. *Would have done,* he said, not *I don't know what I'd do without you.*

"You don't give yourself enough credit, Dad. You'll be fine."

"I certainly will. And that's what I want to talk to you about." He cleared his throat again. "You see, while you were gone, Kaki... She's a very fine woman, Angel."

"She certainly is. The best research assistant I've ever had."

"I'm not talking about her professional qualities. She's warm and giving and kind and witty." Carl ran out of steam. "Altogether a fine woman."

Angel sat back, stunned. She shouldn't be of course. She'd seen them kissing. Still, it was shocking to see her father as flustered as a schoolboy describing his first date. Even more shocking to think of him in a different role from father, teacher, friend.

Furthermore, she'd never seen him at a loss for words. Angel decided to put him out of his misery.

"She is all those things. You must have enjoyed her company while I was gone, and I heartily approve."

"More than that. We fell in love." Carl took his daughter's hand. "I plan to marry her, Angel, and I hope you'll give your blessing."

She sat quietly awhile, absorbing this news. Her dad was obviously elated, and he couldn't have chosen a finer woman. Angel was happy for him, for them. Of course she was.

Change is inevitable, she told herself. The only trouble was that too much change too fast could throw a woman off balance.

"Angel?" Her dad's face was full of concern.

She smiled at him, hoping he wouldn't notice that it was somewhat forced.

"I'm happy for you, Dad. Happy for both of you. I not only approve, but I plan to give the engagement party. When do you want to announce it?"

"We talked some last night and again this morning on the phone, and we decided that since we're planning a big shindig already, we'd announce our plans at the diabetes benefit."

"Marvelous. We'll have the band. We can have a big dance. We'll have the biggest blowout Oxford has ever seen, Dad." She got up to hug her father. "Have you decided what this year's theme is going to be?"

"Yes."

"Come on, Dad. Tell me what it is."

"We've decided to keep it under wraps. All we're saying is that it's going to be casual. And it's going to be a surprise."

"Great. I love surprises."

After Angel went inside to her office, Carl sat in the yard waiting for Kaki.

"You look worried," she said after she'd kissed him.

He drew her onto his lap. "Don't worry, darling, it's not about us. Angel was delighted, as I knew she would be."

"The benefit, then?"

"Yes. Maybe we should go ahead and tell her."

"We talked about this, Carl. Why worry her unnecessarily?"

"True. She has enough on her mind already, and she's started a new book. No need for her to spend two weeks worrying."

They were silent for a while, lost in their separate thoughts. Kaki spoke first.

"Why don't I call the agency this morning and cancel? We'll just have the dance this year."

"No. We've booked the show. There's no way we could get a refund. Besides, there must be dozens of Wild West Shows. What are the chances that this one is Thunderhorse?"

Chapter Fifteen

Steve had always watched the early-morning news before he went to work, and he wasn't about to change his ways now. His jaw clenched as he listened to the latest report.

"The Angel Mercer/Steve Thunderhorse saga continues. We tracked down Angel Mercer at her home in Mississippi, but when questioned about her relationship with the trick rider from Arizona, she issued a terse, "'No comment.'"

Lucas stalked into the kitchen and turned off the TV.

"Why torture yourself?" he said.

"What else is there to do?" Steve handed Lucas a plate.

"You're in a black mood."

"Yes, it's just one of my many charms."

Lucas helped himself to a stack of pancakes with maple syrup, then pulled up a chair to the table.

"I take it you haven't called her yet."

"No, and I don't intend to. The subject is closed."

"Not as long as the media is still jawing about it. Don't they know how to move on to something else?"

"Harping on one note is the style these days. It makes me glad I'm out of the business."

Lucas polished off his pancakes, then poured himself a cup of coffee.

"The agency called the office this morning to remind you about the booking," he said.

"What booking?"

"Didn't you see that notation I put on your calendar?" Steve scowled at him. "Well, I guess not. You were pretty busy. Angel was here."

"Dammit, Lucas." Steve shoved his chair back. "I don't want to hear her name."

Never one to be intimidated or outdone, Lucas shoved his back, too, and stood nose to nose with Steve.

"You can't keep avoiding this, Steve. If you think we're going to walk on eggshells around here, you're mistaken."

Steve ran his hands through his hair. "You're right. I apologize." He rammed his hat on his head. "Finish the rest of the pancakes, Lucas. I know you want them."

"Where are you going?"

"To cancel that booking."

"It's a benefit, Thunderhorse," his agent said over the phone. "You've never let people like this down before. You can't cancel."

Steve looked at the note Lucas had penned on his calendar. "October 17. Wild West Show, Oxford, Mississippi."

Something squeezed his heart.

"Who booked it?" he asked.

There was a pause while Rick Brailey at the agency consulted his notes. "A Ms. Elliott. Ms. Kaki Elliott."

Surely there was no connection. Oxford was a decent-size college town.

"Did she book for herself or for somebody else?"

"She didn't say. Just that it was an annual benefit for diabetes."

Steve could have his agent call and find out, but then what would he do? Cancel? He'd already decided against that.

But he would make damned sure this never happened again. While the Wild West Show had served a noble purpose, it had also served as a means for escape. There would be no more running for Steve.

"No more bookings, Rick."

"This year?"

"Ever."

Thunderhorse hung up and began to make his plans to take his Wild West Show on the road for the last time.

True to their word, Carl and Kaki kept almost every aspect of the annual diabetes benefit a secret.

As a result, excitement was running high in Oxford, and they'd sold more tickets this year than ever before.

Jenny and Britt had arrived yesterday, speaking to each other for a change; Angel's book was going well, and she was surviving. No, better than that. She was learning that broken hearts mend, however slowly.

She no longer burst into tears at the drop of a hat, and the raw ache she'd felt for Steve in the beginning had settled into a constant throb that she could live with.

There was a tap on her bedroom door. "Come in," Angel said.

It was Kaki, looking nervous. And with good reason. The diamond on her finger was as big as an egg, and soon everybody in Oxford would know who had put it there.

Angel finished buttoning her blouse, then grabbed her Stetson and put it on her head at a jaunty angle. "What do you think? Should I wear it tomorrow or not? I'm dying to know about this benefit. Can't you give me a hint?"

"I can do better than that. Sit down, Angel."

She remained standing, but Kaki flopped onto the edge of the bed as if her legs could hardly support her.

"I felt I had to come and tell you this before the show."

"Tell me what?" Angel sat down beside her. "Kaki, what's wrong? This doesn't have anything to do with you and Dad, does it?"

"Not what you're thinking." Kaki's hand was cold as it closed over Angel's. "We planned this benefit while you were in Arizona, before the scandal broke."

Angel's blood suddenly turned to ice, and a sense of foreboding made her shiver.

"What kind of show did you plan, Kaki?"

"A Wild West Show."

A screaming silence filled the room. Angel's bones were too heavy to move. She might have to stay on the edge of the bed forever.

"By the time we found out about you and… We don't know whether he's the one who will be here, Angel. We're hoping not." She squeezed Angel's limp hand. "I meant to call and find out, but I lost my nerve. Anyhow, it was far too late to cancel, so what good would it do to know?

"I feel terrible about this," she added.

"Don't. Is the show already in town?"

"No. The agency said they will arrive this afternoon."

Angel never had to bother with the details of the benefit. Kaki handled everything, including the preshow conference with the performers to make certain that all the events surrounding the benefit ran smoothly.

She always set up a press conference for Angel after the

show, but that could be canceled. In fact, Angel didn't even have to go to the show. She could book a flight to New York, and Kaki could tell the press that Angel was out of town on business.

Jenny could fly there with her. They could spend a few days shopping and talking girl talk, and by the time Angel got back to Oxford the Wild West Show would be gone.

And so would the man doing it.

"You don't have to go, Angel."

Kaki knew her well. Running away had been Angel's style for years. Letting others take care of the messy details. Hiding out.

But that was before she'd gone back to Texas.

"No, Kaki." Angel stood up. "I'm going to the benefit." Having made the brave choice, her courage multiplied. "In fact, I'm going to do better than that. Come down to my office and I'll outline my plan."

The more she thought about her plan, the more she liked it. Forewarned was forearmed.

Besides, didn't Kaki deserve some time to enjoy her engagement?

Oxford, Mississippi, looked like a town that would produce Angel Mercer—gracious, charming, a bit old-fashioned, steeped in rich literary tradition.

After he'd seen to the needs of his horses and his crew, Steve walked to the town square. There on the corner was the bookstore with an enormous display in the window—Angel Mercer, hometown girl, along with copies of all her books.

A life-size cardboard cutout of her dominated the display.

Steve stood on the sidewalk, mesmerized, his heart hurting, his eyes stinging. And all because of a cardboard likeness. If cardboard could put him in such a state, what would the real woman do?

He didn't intend to linger on the streets of Oxford to find out. He was here on business, nothing more. He would go back to his trailer, which served as a temporary office, meet with this Ms. Kaki Elliott, then do the show and get the hell out of Dodge.

The knock on his door sounded at precisely four o'clock. Ms. Elliott was prompt, Steve would grant her that.

"Come in," he said, and Angel Mercer walked through the door.

"It *is* you," she said.

Shocked, silent, staring, Steve was torn between the desire to kiss her and the need to run. God, a woman had no right to look so appealing. She hovered near the doorway, a vision in white, her blond hair loose and flowing over her shoulders, her lips parted in surprise, her fragrance filling his nostrils, her very essence seeping into his soul.

Coward that he was, he took refuge behind the desk.

"I would ask you to sit down, but I have a four-o'clock appointment."

"I *am* your four-o'clock appointment."

She chose a chair as far away from him as possible. The distance didn't lessen her impact one bit. He still wanted to throw her over his shoulder like some savage and find a cave somewhere to keep her captive for the next few centuries.

Instead, he sat in the chair facing her. Looking calmer than he felt, he hoped.

"You used an alias?"

"No. Kaki Elliott is my research assistant. She handles all details of these annual diabetes benefits...until today."

He didn't know how it could be possible, but she was lovelier than he remembered.

Her dress looked like something made of moonbeams. Was it the same one she'd worn in Arizona? The one that drove him mad? The one that still drove him mad, just thinking about it.

Had she worn it deliberately? Did she remember, too?

"I want you to know that I had nothing to do with bringing you here to Oxford," she said.

"I know you didn't."

The call had come while she was still in Arizona, but he didn't say that. Seeing her was painful enough without bringing up a subject that would exacerbate the pain.

"I didn't know anything about the Wild West Show until today."

"And I didn't know you were the benefactress. I should have guessed of course. It was all too coincidental."

They got caught up in each other, eyes locked, hearts pounding double time. Sweat popped out on his brow, but he'd be damned if he would wipe it off. It was bad enough that he could barely control his desire.

Did she notice? Was the same fire sweeping through her veins? Did she want him as much as he wanted her?

She wet her lips with a tongue as pink as sugar candy. The small gesture almost drove him wild.

"Is everything all set for the show?" she said.

"Yes. You'll get your show, Angel."

It was the first time since she'd walked into his temporary office that Steve had said her name.

The way he said it, like a caress, was almost more than Angel could bear. She had been foolish coming here, foolish to think she could face him so easily, foolish to think she could keep things between them strictly business.

Her heart refused to be tamed. It was hammering so hard she thought it would beat right out of her chest.

Her body refused to be subdued. It was in total riot, blood boiling, skin sensitized, legs weak.

Why hadn't she let Kaki do this? Or at the very least, why hadn't she stayed home and simply called him on the phone?

Because I wanted to see him.

There was no denying the truth. She'd wanted desperately to see him, to touch him, to love him.

Oh, God, how she wanted to love him.

That was impossible of course. He'd walked out on her. She'd have to remember that.

"I'm waiving my fee." He held up his hand to stop her protest. "I've instructed my agent to return your check."

"That's very generous. Thank you. You have the complete schedule?"

"Yes."

"You and your crew are welcome at all events."

"Thank you."

So stiff. So formal. How had the two of them come so far from the quick hot embraces and sizzling passion of Arizona?

"The show is not really the reason I came here today. Kaki could have handled that."

He waited. Icy. Self-contained. Distant. Angel wanted to scream.

"The press will descend on Oxford full force for this event," she said. "They always do."

"They'll have a field day with this."

"That's why I came. So we could decide the best way to handle the press."

"I plan to avoid them. It won't be so easy for you."

"It will be impossible. The only way I can avoid the press is to leave town, and I don't plan on doing that."

Was that the ghost of a smile she saw? And what did it mean?

Nothing, she told herself. Steve Thunderhorse's smile meant nothing, his gestures meant nothing, his presence meant nothing except that he was here to do business.

She'd do well to remember that.

"If you say nothing to the press, they will speculate endlessly, then draw their own conclusions, mostly false."

That smile again. "I believe they've already done that, Angel. There's nothing more they can do to me."

A sudden anger overtook her, stunning in its force.

"What about me, Steve? Or doesn't that matter? You're so wrapped up in your own pain, your own past, that you don't care what happens to me."

The minute the words were out of her mouth, she wanted to call them back. But it was too late, far too late. His eyes turned so black they looked like burning coals in his tight face.

"I'm sorry," she whispered. "I shouldn't have said that."

Pantherlike, he came to her, dark, brooding, intense. When he was standing beside her chair, she could hardly breathe. He stood there for a small eternity, looking down at her, his face filled with yearning.

She wanted to weep. For herself. For him. For the promise they lost.

"I care, Angel." When his hand touched her hair, she died inside. Bending over, he touched the single strand of hair to his lips. "Believe me, I care."

Love me, her heart cried. *Love me.*

Still and silent, she watched him walk back to his chair.

"Tell me," he said. "What is your plan for dealing with the press?"

"Kaki is scheduling a press conference for ten o'clock tomorrow morning. At my house, in my office."

"Smart move. Being on your own turf gives you the advantage."

"I would like you to be there."

"No."

"Why not?"

"As I said before, there's nothing more they can do to me."

"But don't you want to set the record straight?"

"No. I left the rat race years ago, Angel. I understand why you need to make certain that there is not too much negative fallout from the publicity surrounding you. I applaud your spunk and your courage."

He left his desk, poured two cups of coffee and handed one to her, careful not to linger over the brief touch of their hands.

"I just thought that if both of us denied any personal connection, the impact would be greater."

"Is that what you plan to do, Angel? Deny any personal connection to me?"

Was that pain she was hearing? Wounded pride? A little nostalgia, perhaps?

"Yes," she said.

A heavy silence filled the room. Steve sipped his coffee, his face revealing nothing.

What was he thinking? She'd give everything she possessed to know.

"It's true, isn't it, Steve? We have no personal connection."

For a moment his control slipped, and she caught a

glimpse of agony. Then the mask was back in place, and she was left to wonder if she'd been mistaken.

"I think that's what you should tell the press, Angel, that we have no personal connection."

He didn't deny it. Was that because he couldn't? Was that because his heart was still entwined with hers?

Somewhere deep inside a tiny seed of hope was planted. After all, she believed in miracles. Was it too much to expect one for herself?

"I want to put an end to these rumors," she said. "That's all."

"That's a worthy goal. I think you should pursue it."

She didn't know the man who sat so stiffly on his chair. Like one of the wooden Indians that used to stand in front of barbershops in small-town America.

She wanted to shake him out of his complacency. She wanted to stir something in him, some spark of emotion, longing, regret, even anger. Anything to get him to drop that awful mask and look at her as Steve Thunderhorse.

"And what is your goal, Steve? To run away?"

His smile was sardonic. "Bravo, Angel. Lucas would approve."

Still, he remained cool, detached. Angel could no longer bear to be in this cramped space with him. She could hardly breathe. She thought her heart was about to quit beating.

Standing, she put an official end to the torture.

"I think it best that for the duration of your stay in Oxford, we avoid seeing each other except in public."

She paused, waiting for him to agree, disagree, protest, take her in his arms and kiss her. Anything. Anything except this awful cold silence.

He merely stared at her, inscrutable.

"You are and your crew are, of course, invited to all

events surrounding the show—the barbecue, the moonlight dinner and dance.''

''Thank you.''

Did that mean he would come? He wouldn't come? All this uncertainty was giving her a headache.

''Thank you for coming, Steve. I know you're going to make this benefit a great success.''

''Anything for a worthy cause.'' He held the door open for her. ''Goodbye, Angel.''

She didn't cry until she was halfway home, then she pulled her car off the road, laid her head on the steering wheel and wept her heart out.

Chapter Sixteen

An hour before the press conference, Kaki and Carl slipped out the back door with Angel's blessing.

"Keep him at your house, Kaki," Angel said.

"My pleasure." Kaki beamed and so did Carl. Lately Angel had started referring to them as the lovebirds, but not without cost. Only a few weeks ago she could have been dubbed one of a pair.

"Don't go anywhere that reporters can waylay you. I'll call and let you know when the press conference is over."

"I hate to leave you alone," her dad said, always the worrier.

"Don't worry. Jenny and Britt will be here any minute." She kissed his cheek, then Kaki's. "Take care, you two."

He dad chucked her under the chin. "Remember, sweetheart, you're a champ."

They were holding hands when they walked toward the

car, and when they drove off, Kaki at the wheel, they were smiling.

"If anybody tries to ruin this time for them, I'll coat them with peanut butter and hang them out for the birds."

The house was strangely quiet after they left. "This is what it will be like after they're married and gone," Angel said.

One person in a great big house, rattling around in too much space and with too much time on her hands.

"You should move to New York after the big event," Jenny had told her last week. "The change of pace might be good for you, and we'd have a blast together."

Angel couldn't imagine herself living anywhere except Mississippi...or Arizona. With Thunderhorse so close, the ranch and all it had meant to them was very much on her mind.

The sound of a car rescued her from another bout of weeping. It would be Jenny and Britt, coming early for a strategy session before the press conference.

Angel went out onto the front porch to greet them. "Only one car?" she said.

"He drives like a maniac. I ought to have my head examined."

Britt flashed his award-winning smile. "You should have your head examined, but not because of my driving, cupcake."

"If you call me that again, I'm going to throw up."

"I'll get the barf bag," Britt said.

Their banter was mostly good-natured, very familiar and extremely comforting. Angel hugged them both.

"Thank you for coming."

"If you think I'm going to let you face the wolves alone, you've got another think coming." Jenny tossed her purse onto the floor, then sat down and kicked off her shoes.

Britt threw his head back and did a mock howl. "Somebody put a muzzle on him," Jenny complained, but she was smiling.

Suddenly Britt became all business. "This is a good idea, Angel, taking an offensive position, instead of waiting to be put on the defensive." He opened his briefcase. "Is Thunderhorse coming?"

"No. He said he left the rat race years ago."

Britt was lost in thought for a while. "He's either the smartest man I've ever known or the most foolish."

Angel swallowed a lump in her throat. Jenny was quick to the rescue.

"Hey, where's the coffee and doughnuts? The best thing to do to a pack of wolves is feed them."

"In the kitchen," Angel said.

"I'll be right back, if you two think you can carry on without me."

Britt reached for Angel's hand. "You're cold. Nervous?"

"A little bit."

"Don't be. I'm here to make sure that this conference goes the way you want it to, Angel."

"You know the right questions to ask?"

"I'll not only ask the right questions, I'll dominate the conference so that nobody else can ask the wrong ones." He gave her a lopsided smile. "It'll be the first time in my long and illustrious career that I've soft-pedaled an interview."

"You don't know how much I appreciate what you're doing for me. I don't want you to compromise your ethics, though."

Britt turned deadly serious. "Think of it as me taking a stand against sensationalism. It's time we stopped crucifying our public figures in the media."

Jenny bustled through the door and he took the coffee she offered.

"I could get to admire this Thunderhorse if I'm not careful," he said.

Angel got misty and Jenny elbowed him. "Did anybody ever tell you that you talk too much?"

"That's what I do best, cupcake. More's the pity."

If Angel didn't know better, she'd say that Britt and Jenny had called a truce. She didn't have time to ponder the question, for the television news crew pulled into her driveway.

Jenny fussed with Angel's hair. "Go get 'em, champ."

Steve sat in his trailer nursing a headache, a cup of coffee and a bad mood. The television on the edge of his desk was ancient, the screen so small he needed a magnifying glass to make out the details. But the reception was good and the picture was in color.

Angel looked stunning in red. The color of power. The color of passion.

He would hate to be in the reporters' place. Apparently it was easy enough to cast stones at an absent target, but when the target was so enticing, casting them was much harder.

"Smart move, Angel," he said. But then, he'd always known she was smart. That was one of the things he admired most about her—her intelligence, her intellectual curiosity.

The camera panned in for a close-up. Steve knew the routine. First there would be the prepared statement, then questions, monitored by the woman beside her—Jenny Cordova, her agent, according to the information that flashed across the screen.

He turned up the volume as Angel began to read.

"I've asked you here today to clarify a personal matter

that has recently been the subject of speculation, innuendo and outright lies.''

Angel paused to level an artless smile at the camera.

For a moment Steve was speechless. He'd never expected such a strong statement from such a fragile-looking woman. And he'd be willing to bet that neither had anybody else in that room.

''Bravo, Angel,'' he cheered.

''Sometime ago,'' she continued, ''I was accosted by a tourist wielding a camera as I attempted to enjoy a quiet evening meal. If she had approached me in a polite manner and asked that I pose for a photograph, I would gladly have obliged. Instead, she and her husband stalked me in a manner that was not only invasive, but also frightening.''

Angel paused to let the effect of her words sink in. The camera panned in close, and Steve could actually see a residual fear in her eyes. On camera, Angel Mercer looked like a delicate hummingbird caught in a trap.

Clenching his hands into fists, he called himself every kind of coward. He should be there at her side today, protecting her, defending her honor.

''I was with a friend that evening,'' Angel said, ''a very fine man who breeds and trains horses in Arizona. If there was ever a man who exemplifies the term *hero,* it is Steve Thunderhorse.''

''Don't, Angel,'' Steve whispered, but of course she didn't hear. ''Don't pin any medals on me.''

''Seeing that I was close to hysteria, he picked me up and bodily carried me out of the restaurant, and that, ladies and gentlemen, is the picture that made headlines around the world—a gallant man rescuing a frightened woman.''

The camera panned in on Jenny Cordova. ''We'll take questions now.'' A general hubbub erupted, and Jenny held up her hands. "One at a time, please." She nodded toward Britt Ace. "Mr. Ace?"

"Miss Mercer, how would you characterize your relationship with Steve Thunderhorse?"

"We are friends, that's all."

Her words were arrows, piercing Steve's heart. He gripped his coffee cup so hard it was a wonder the ceramic didn't crack.

"In fact," Angel continued, "he has graciously agreed to donate his time and talent for the diabetes benefit I sponsor each year."

A reporter yelled from the back, "Is he here now?"

Jenny Cordova answered with a terse yes, then, "Next question? Mr. Ace…"

It was unusual, Thunderhorse thought, that she would grant him two questions in a row, especially with a roomful of eager reporters.

"Are you personally acquainted with his history, and what do you have to say in response to the comments of his ex-wife?"

Jenny smiled. "That's two questions, Mr. Ace."

"Sorry."

He didn't look sorry. In fact, the famous Britt Ace was looking smug and rather pleased with himself. It didn't take Steve long to figure out the truth: Jenny Cordova and Britt Ace, and perhaps Angel, too, were in cahoots. Furthermore, the point of the conference seemed more to exonerate Thunderhorse than to squelch rumors.

"Yes, I know of his past," Angel was saying, "and I can think of nothing more tragic than to lose a child to a random act of violence. I don't know how I would have handled such a tragedy, do you?"

Without using the word *alcoholic,* Angel had effectively put a different light on all the bad press. The pain of loss almost overwhelmed Steve—loss of Sunny, loss of Emily, loss of Angel.

He wanted desperately to turn off the set, to shut out the truth, but he sat mesmerized as Angel continued talking.

"I can tell you this—Steve Thunderhorse is respected, generous, productive, successful and sober. He and Emily Thunderhorse suffered a terrible loss, and they deserve compassion, not excoriation."

"Next question?" Jenny said.

She looked in Britt's direction again, but a female reporter on the front row burst out, "What about Emily Thunderhorse's accusation that her ex-husband is a gold digger?"

Jenny started to brush her off, but Angel put a restraining hand on her arm.

"Generous successful men don't indulge in that activity."

"But what about Emily—"

Angel smoothly interrupted her. "Emily Thunderhorse deserves to be left in peace to deal with whatever ghosts still haunt her."

Then she turned a megawatt smile on the gathering. "Thank you for coming. I hope to see all of you at the benefit, and I hope you'll be generous with your donations of time and money to our worthy cause."

Reporters fired desperate questions from the back, but Jenny Cordova took the floor.

"No more questions. This press conference is over."

The regular programming came back on, a game show with an overly enthusiastic host and two leggy blond assistants with false eyelashes and false smiles.

Steve left the game show on. Anything to fill the void left by Angel. Anything to keep his mind off the truth.

Angel's final assessment of Emily haunted Steve, that she should be left in peace to deal with her ghosts.

"You've got to deal with it," Lucas had told him years

ago when he'd come to D.C. and found Steve dead drunk, lying in a filthy bed that hadn't been changed in weeks. "Sunny's dead, and I'm not going to let you die, too."

What would Steve have done without Lucas? Would he still be in Washington, D.C., going from bar to bar trying to drown his sorrows?

And what of Emily? In recent interviews she had accused him of abandonment, and he had labeled her bitter and unfair and vindictive.

But did she have a point?

There was a knock on the trailer door.

"Come in."

Wayne entered, dripping with sweat. "Damn, it's hot in Mississippi. Eighty degrees in October. I never heard of such a thing."

"Welcome to hell," Steve said.

"I see your mood hasn't improved since we left Arizona."

"It must be the weather."

"Yeah, well…I thought I'd check out that barbecue this afternoon. The locals have been telling me that some of the best barbecue in the world is right here in Oxford, Mississippi."

"Check it out."

"Are you coming?"

"I don't think so." Wayne gave him a look. He was getting as bad as Lucas about being an old mother hen. "I have lots to do to get ready for the show."

"Hey, I'll stay here and help you. No problem."

"No. Go ahead and enjoy yourself. There's nothing I can't handle alone."

Alone. That's how he preferred to be. Wasn't it?

Chapter Seventeen

Steve wasn't coming.

Angel tried not to be obvious as she scanned the afternoon crowd for the heartachingly familiar sight of a tall dark-eyed man who looked as if he'd been carved in bronze.

Jenny came up beside her, plate stacked with barbecued ribs, baked beans and coleslaw. "Lord, I could eat my weight in this stuff." She twirled around to show off her tight designer jeans and western-style shirt. "Do you think I'm getting fat?"

"Barbie dolls would drool with envy."

"Truly?"

"You look fabulous, as always. What's all this sudden concern over how you look, Jenny?" Jenny developed an acute interest in her ribs. "You sly dog. It's a man. You've found somebody."

"No, not really."

Before Angel could pursue that line of questioning, Britt

joined them. "My compliments, Angel. This is much better than last year's overcooked steak and half-done potatoes."

Angel laughed. "Thanks, I guess. It was all Dad and Kaki's doings."

"Did anybody ever tell you that you're the soul of tact, Britt? You've got sauce on your chin." Jenny stood on tiptoe and wiped it off with her napkin.

"There are better ways of doing that, cupcake."

"If you call me that again—"

"I know, you're going to turn me loose among the panting coeds." Laughing, Britt linked his arm through Jenny's. "Come on, let's check out that lemonade stand. Coming, Angel?"

"No, you two go ahead. I have something I need to do."

It wasn't a lie, exactly. It was more of a smokescreen. That something involved walking the entire perimeter of the football field, searching for signs of a familiar Sioux.

Assaulted by the unseasonable heat and the smells of barbecue, Steve searched the crowd for one face, the face he couldn't get out of his mind no matter how hard he tried.

He knew he shouldn't have come. Nothing had changed for him, not the past, not Emily's hatred, not his own determination to avoid any future entanglements that would test his power to protect.

And yet, he had to see Angel. Merely see her.

Suddenly there she was, hat in her hand, pink dress billowing around her slender form, moving waiflike through the crowd. Head and shoulders above most of the people there, he had no trouble seeing her. He leaned against the trunk of an ancient magnolia tree and watched as she stopped to pet a dog, to touch a small child's hand, to speak to the people who had come to support her favorite charity.

She was exquisitely beautiful, smiling, self-confident.

That was what any person watching her would see. But Steve was not seeing with his eyes; he was seeing with his heart. And what he saw was a melancholy that matched his own, an ineffable sadness that nothing could alleviate.

Glancing in his direction, her eyes swept the crowd, then stopped, locked on his. For a moment the old familiar spark came into her eyes, and then it faded as quickly as it had come.

Turning her face from him, Angel walked away, and his heart knew more regret than a heart could hold.

"Angel, wait."

Without thought, without a plan, Steve strode through the crowd. He knew only one thing. He had to be with Angel, if only for a moment.

As he gained on her from behind, he glimpsed a reporter closing in on her from the left. Steve quickened his pace, but he was not fast enough.

The thick dark man with a camera slung over his shoulder and a press badge pinned on his sweat-soaked shirt arrived first.

"Miss Mercer, may I have a moment?"

"Certainly." Ever gracious, Angel turned around. "Mr. Glendenning from Atlanta, isn't it?"

"I'm flattered."

"You were at the press conference this morning."

"Yes, I was." He unstrapped his camera. "May I? To go with the lead about the benefit."

"Certainly."

Feeling foolish, Steve lingered in the background. All his anxiety had been for nothing. Angel was bound to be plagued by reporters wherever she went, most of them with no more motive than to get a good shot for the story.

What he should do was steal quietly back to his makeshift

office and forget he'd ever come to the barbecue, forget he'd ever seen an angelic woman dressed in pink.

He had turned to go when Glendenning of Atlanta went in for the kill.

"Now, Miss Mercer—" the reporter was suddenly in her face, jabbing his finger at her "—what were you and Thunderhorse doing together up there at the Paradise Ranch?"

"How did—"

"Angel, don't." Steve stepped in front of her, shielding her from the reporter. "Miss Mercer made her statement to the press this morning. She has no further comment."

"My God! Thunderhorse!"

Glendenning had his camera up, snapping shots as fast as the shutter would move.

Steve moved fast, jostling Glendenning so the camera fell to the ground.

"Sorry. Let me get that."

Glendenning was no match for Steve. Six inches shorter and fifty pounds heavier, he was still huffing and puffing while Steve knelt, jerked the film out of the camera, then handed it back to the reporter.

"You son of a—"

Steve grabbed his arm. "Remember your manners, Mr. Glendenning. There are women and children present." Still holding the man's arm, he steered him toward the privacy of a copse of trees.

"Now, do you want to tell me how you knew about Paradise Ranch, or do you want to spend the next few months with that finger you were jabbing at Angel Mercer in a sling?"

"Are you threatening me?"

"No. I just asked you a polite question. Two, as a matter of fact."

"I never reveal my sources. You, of all people, ought to know that."

Steve was so enraged that he actually could have broken the man's arm. And more. The force of his fury shook his beliefs about himself.

He had thought that being on the ranch for nine years had leached all the hatred out of him. He had believed that living in peaceful surroundings had made him a peaceful man, a man who could stand aside and look at life in amusement. He had thought he would never again care so deeply for a woman that the sight of her face on the television screen would move him to tears, that the sight of her tears would move him to compassion, that the sight of her fear would move him to rage.

He had thought himself immune to life, safe from love.

And he had been wrong.

The stench of Glendenning's fear made him sick. The man himself made him sick.

"Mr. Glendenning, you've worn out your welcome in Oxford. I suggest you go home."

"I'll have you up on charges for this."

Over the reporter's shoulder, Steve spotted Angel, wide-eyed and distraught. Abruptly he released the reporter.

"You might want to rethink that, Mr. Glendenning," Angel said as she moved to stand beside Steve. "There could be some question about who was making the threats and who suffered severe emotional trauma."

Glendenning slunk off, and Steve was left with Angel. He wanted nothing more than to take her in his arms and hold her, merely hold her. But a crowd of many hundreds milled just beyond view.

"I don't think he'll bother you again. In fact, I suspect he's already booking a flight home."

Angel made a choked sound like a fawn in distress and

looked at him with big wet eyes. Steve put his arm around her shoulders and guided her toward his rented car.

When they were seated inside, she murmured, "The crowd…"

"Damn the crowd."

"The reporters."

"Damn them, too."

"Steve, where are you going?"

"Does it matter?"

"No."

Thankfully, no members of the press saw them leave.

"Where do you live, Angel?"

"On Lamar."

"Give me directions."

"You can't—"

"Give me directions, Angel."

This time she didn't argue. Steve drove in silence, concentrating on the town, the trees, the streets, anything except the woman sitting beside him—and his motives.

What was she doing in the car with Steve Thunderhorse? Angel wondered. What was she doing sitting in the passenger seat pretending that it was perfectly normal to be going to her house with the man who had jilted her?

So there it was. The truth. At last.

Steve Thunderhorse had jilted her. He'd left her standing in his bedroom without giving her a chance to talk about their relationship. He'd been as protective as a mother hen, then had left her to drive home alone without another thought.

This was the first time she'd let herself be angry, and it felt good. Cathartic.

"I don't know what you're trying to prove with these caveman tactics," she said.

Her anger caught him off guard. His surprise showed in his face. Good. It was about time somebody got underneath that careful mask he wore.

"I'm not trying to prove anything, Angel. I'm taking you home. That's all."

"Why?"

"You know the answer to that."

"No, I don't. Illuminate me."

"You're hounded by the press at every turn. More than hounded. Harassed. Threatened."

"And you think I can't take care of myself."

"I didn't say that."

"No, but that's the way you're acting."

The silence was so thick you could have cut it with a knife. Steve drove with his jaw clenched, and Angel sat beside him boiling with silent rage.

A woman rejected. That vision gave her a certain amount of perverse satisfaction. She felt like one of her own characters, a woman full of motives, taking center stage, commanding the scene.

"And another thing," she said. "Why did you come to the barbecue?"

"You invited me."

"I invited you to eat, not to manhandle me."

"I think you have me confused with Glendenning of Atlanta."

He stared resolutely ahead, as if the road they were traveling required his undivided attention. Angel wanted to hit something. Instead, she retreated into an aggrieved silence.

"Which house is yours?"

"The yellow one."

Steve pulled into the driveway and cut the engine. It didn't take long for the car to heat up inside. Not that it wasn't already heated from the sheer force of their disagreements.

"I guess you expect me to invite you in," she said, feeling petty and mean and ungracious and perfectly justified.

"No."

He leaned across her lap to open her door, his chest so close she could feel his body heat, his arm grazing her legs, heating her skin to the point of combustion. Angel sucked in a sharp breath.

Steve shot her a piercing look, and she knew that he saw right through her, saw through the sham of her rage, the pretense of her indifference, saw right to the heart of the truth.

Angel wet her dry lips with the tip of her tongue. Sweat beaded her upper lip and shivers ran down her spine.

Get out of the car, she told herself silently. She was in no condition to deal with this man.

Instead, she sat mesmerized, unwilling to give up one second of being near the man she had loved, the man she still loved.

"Angel."

That was all he said, just "Angel," and suddenly she was back in Arizona, back in the time of careless bliss when she'd squandered precious minutes sleeping, instead of making memories for the bleak time ahead.

What, Steve? What? she wanted to ask. Instead, she was silent, barely breathing as his gaze swept over her face, lingering on her lips until they trembled.

Desire rose quickly between them, as it always had, and the air in the car became hot, charged, almost unbearable.

"You're hot," he said.

His voice was low and seductive, though not intentionally. Or was it? Was he playing some wicked game with her, a game whose rules she didn't know?

She had to get out of the car before it was too late. Suddenly his hands were on her face, and it was already too late. Softly he gathered the moisture from her upper lip with his fingertips.

She felt like a starving traveler who had stumbled into a banquet hall. His touch felt so good she wanted to hold it there forever.

Her lips parted and his finger slid inside her mouth. Did she do that, or did he? It didn't matter. Nothing mattered except the rush of pleasure. With exquisite tenderness she licked away the moisture that tasted of salt and regret.

Everything about the moment was burned into her memory—the hot car seat pressing into her back, the way his eyes darkened with desire, the empty ache in her heart. She couldn't let him go.

Not now. Not yet.

He moved away from her and there was nothing except the car door, swung wide open, and beyond, the walkway that led to her empty house.

"You didn't eat at the picnic," she said.

"No."

"Come inside. I'll feed you."

Chapter Eighteen

There was something unsettling about seeing Steve in her house, as if his very presence had rearranged her furniture, rehung the draperies and redecorated her living room. Everything looked brand-new to her, and suddenly she realized that she was seeing her house through his eyes.

"You have a pretty house," he said. "Like you."

"Thank you."

She hugged the compliment to herself, knowing that later when she lay in bed alone she would remember every word he'd said, mull them over, analyze them, replay them like a broken record.

He followed her into the kitchen where she made two ham sandwiches with mustard.

"My specialty," she said, grinning wryly. "I'm not much of a cook."

"I remember."

So did she. She remembered everything about their time

together in Arizona, including every word he'd ever said to her. She'd loved his stories, the way he had of squinting his eyes as he recalled in perfect detail how the sun had cast diamonds across the water as it rose over the Verde River, the way a newborn colt looked when it took its first wobbly steps, or the way a pair of eagles flew underneath their young on their maiden journey, wings outspread.

Steve Thunderhorse had one of the best minds she'd ever encountered. He was not only intelligent, but full of intellectual curiosity. Learning was intense pleasure for him. His house was filled with books. She'd browsed through the titles the day she discovered the sunny room that would be perfect for writing.

They were so good together. But he had thrown it all away. *Why?* she wanted to scream at him. Why?

Instead, she offered him lemonade.

"Most people drink coffee this time of year," she said, "but I prefer lemonade. Especially when the weather is unseasonably hot."

Chattering. That wasn't like her at all.

She took a fortifying drink from her glass, but all the while she was picturing how Steve's toothbrush would look next to hers, how she would love to wake up in the morning and find his shaving cream side by side with her bath powder, how she'd enjoy walking into her closet and seeing his boots among her shoes, his shirts mixed in with hers, his jeans making her closet look masculine and important.

So this is love.

Not just the passion, the quick hot desire that sent them tumbling to the nearest available surface. But the soft imaginings, the shared plans, the dreams.

"Thanks for the sandwich," he said, standing.

He was going. Just like that.

"Steve."

"Yes?"

"In the car...I'm sorry I was so mad."

"Don't be. I'm sorry if I seemed high-handed."

"Seemed?" She laughed. "You *were*."

"I know I have no right to interfere..." The look he gave her was full of things neither of them could say. "You should be more careful, Angel. You are one of the new breed—a celebrity writer. What happened this afternoon is going to be repeated. And it could get worse."

"I can't stay locked inside my house. I *refuse* to."

"Then perhaps you should think about hiring someone to be with you when you're in public."

"A bodyguard? You've got to be kidding."

"You're not taking this seriously."

"I might as well be in prison if I'm to have somebody dogging my steps all the time."

"Why are you being so stubborn, Angel?"

"Why are you?"

Her voice was raised, her back was stiff and her head was beginning to hurt. Love hurt. It was a revelation to her.

Steve didn't answer her question. Was it because he couldn't? Or he wouldn't?

"I won't always be there to protect you," he said.

"Who asked you to? As I recall, you're the one who walked out."

There. At last she'd said it, the accusation she'd been dying to fling at him ever since he'd come to Oxford.

"Things aren't always what they seem, Angel."

His calmness stoked her fires, all of them—her passion, her anger, her weepiness.

"Don't spout platitudes at me, Steve Thunderhorse. Be specific. You're a writer."

"Not anymore."

He turned to leave. If he went out that door without saying another word, he was never coming back. Never. But if he turned, if only for a second, there was hope.

Only the desperate played such games, and Angel figured she was reduced to desperation.

He went through the kitchen door, and she heard his footsteps as he vanished down the hall.

Good manners dictated that she accompany him to the front door. She stayed in the kitchen.

"Let him find his own way out," she muttered.

His footsteps got louder, and suddenly he was there, standing in her kitchen doorway, his pain clearly stamped on his face.

She called on every bit of willpower she possessed to keep from running to him.

"I forgot to thank you for the sandwich," he said.

"You're welcome."

Still, he lingered in the doorway. Her heart yearned for him, but she kept her distance. A half-mended heart, broken once more, might never recover.

Any minute now he would leave again. She couldn't bear it. She had to get him to stay, if only for a little while. Suddenly it came to her.

"Steve, there's something I forgot. Will you follow me?"

She led the way toward her office on the sunny side of the house where light poured into the room and every window offered a view of the flower gardens. Steve's gaze scanned her mahogany bookcases, her Queen Anne desk with the Oriental rug underneath, her collection of jade elephants and music boxes from around the world.

She knew what he was doing—taking her measure through her workplace. It was the same thing she'd done at his house.

Reaching for her favorite music box, the crystal ball with a bright blue dragon inside, she wound it up and set it to playing "Camelot." She knew the words, and as the tinkling sounds of music filled the room she thought about the phrase "happily ever aftering," and her heart was filled with sadness.

"Nice office," he said, his gaze moving from her face to the books she'd written.

"I'll give you a signed copy."

She pulled her first Muriel book from the shelves and scrawled her name and the date across the page. No greeting, no catchy phrases, no best wishes or warm regards. Just *Angel Mercer,* the *A* and the *M* made larger by her nervousness, the endings almost indecipherable.

When he took the book, their hands touched briefly. Was it for that small touch she'd given him the book? No, there was something more. She wanted to think of her book lying on his bedside table, to think of him picking it up at random moments, the first thing every morning, the last thing every night. She wanted to imagine him tracing her signature with his fingertips, turning to her photo on the jacket and gazing at her with longing and nostalgia.

She wanted him to remember.

"Thank you, Angel."

Was that all, then? Just *Thank you?* For once she wished he wasn't such a man of few words.

Then, "I'll treasure the book…always."

Something inside her relaxed. That was more like it, she thought.

She gave him her most radiant smile, the one reserved for special people, and they stood in her office staring at each other, the air as thick as honey.

"I should be going," he said, reluctant, it seemed. Or was it her foolish imagination?

He was already at the door when it occurred to her why she'd brought him there in the first place.

"Wait," she said. "You must think I'm the most arrogant person in the world, bringing you in here to give you one of my books."

"No, I don't think that at all."

What, Steve? What do you think? Do I still appeal to you? Does your blood heat when you look at me the way mine does when I look at you? Do you long to touch me, to hug me, to hold me, merely hold me so that we can both know we're not alone?

What?

"I came in here for the specific purpose of writing you a check," she said.

"I'm donating my time for the Wild West Show. I thought I'd made that perfectly clear."

"Yes, well…this is not about the show."

She moistened her lips with the tip of her tongue, loving the way his face changed as he watched her. Was she deliberately flirting with him? She thought so. What woman wouldn't? He was the most appealing man she'd ever known, and she was no plaster saint. She wasn't above stooping to a few dirty tactics to get what she wanted, or at least to make him regret what he didn't have.

"It's about your camper. I damaged it."

"I remember."

They got caught up once more in memories, caught up in each other.

"I forgot to write you a check," she said.

"I don't want your money."

"I always pay my debts."

"I won't accept money from you."

He was stubborn; she was willful. He was unmovable; she was determined.

Could nothing make a dent in his cool facade?

"What will you accept from me, Steve? What do you want from me?"

Her question scored a direct hit. Steve looked at if he'd been punched in the gut.

"For payment?" His voice was a knife blade, sharp, dangerous.

"Yes."

"For the camper?"

"For the camper…for everything."

"You want to buy me off, to square all debts, to make certain there are no loose ends that might be construed as *personal involvement?*"

"Yes," she whispered.

A north wind blew across her heart, and she shuddered. This is how the rival tribes must have felt when the Sioux were on the warpath, she thought.

He stalked her, his eyes hawklike, seeing right through her sham.

"This," he said.

Swift as an eagle he pulled her into a hard embrace. She struggled briefly, but it was useless. She might as well have been shoving against a mountain.

"What do you think you're doing?"

He didn't answer her. Instead, he tightened his hold. He was so close she could feel the steady beat of his heart against hers, smell the clean soap and fresh-air scent of his skin, see the thick dark hair that curled just beneath the V where his shirt buttoned.

The fight went out of her. There was no use pretending, anyway. She was exactly where she wanted to be, and Steve knew it.

Let him make what he would of it. Let him take advantage. Let him pick her up and storm toward her bedroom where he would hold her captive for the next few days, the next few years, the next few centuries.

He bent down to rest his lips against her hair. A small sigh escaped her.

"You smell good," he said.

"You *feel* good."

She snuggled closer, beginning to sway now with the rightness of the thing, the absolutely perfect pattern of this embrace.

He leaned back to smile down at her. "There's not enough hugging in this world."

Angel thought it was the most beautiful thing she'd ever heard. How could she bear to let this man go?

She glanced at the bentwood rocker in the corner of her office. She was the kind of woman who kept rocking chairs all over the house, her philosophy being that a rocking chair added warmth to a room and made a person feel welcome.

"I would love to sit in that chair and have you hold me," she whispered.

Without a word Steve scooped her up and sat in the rocking chair, arranging her in his lap as if she were made of spun glass, precious and breakable.

"There," he said. "Is that better?"

"Much."

She buried her face in the crook of his shoulder, inhaling deeply. She would never forget the scent of this man. It was seared into her mind along with the imprint of his body. Even alone in the dark she could perfectly recall every detail of his body, down to the tiny mole at the base of his left hip.

Steve began to rock and Angel let herself dream. Just for a little while. Just long enough to store this, the most precious memory of all.

She dreamed not of the past but of the future, of the two

of them together in Arizona, surrounded by the endurable—mountains and canyons and the river that ran through it all. She dreamed of good friends, Lucas and Jenny and Britt and Wayne, their lives woven like bright threads through the skein of hers. She dreamed of children and grandchildren and great grandchildren, generations of Thunderhorses bearing Steve's genes and hers, mixed forever in love. And dreaming, she slept.

Steve saw the droop of her eyelids, felt her slump against him, boneless and content. And his heart broke in two.

"I'm sorry, Angel." He pressed his lips into her hair, inhaling the soft sweet fragrance of her. "I never meant to hurt you. I never meant to leave you."

Her lips curved into a soft smile, as if she'd heard him. Or was she merely dreaming?

"I meant to be with you forever, to love you and protect you."

An image came to him, a little girl with dark curls and a smile that would melt your heart. The casket had been so tiny, the grave so small.

The pain so great.

Angel sighed, a long exhalation of breath as she dropped into deep sleep. She must be exhausted. The strain of playing hostess to hundreds at the annual benefit added to the constant strain of being on public display.

He would give everything he owned if he could spare her that burden, if he could love her and protect her forever.

But the risk of loving was too great, the price of losing too high.

Steve shifted so he could see Angel's face. He wanted to memorize every line, every soft curve—the lips that were slightly heart-shaped, the downy cheeks that looked like ripe peaches, the long sweep of her eyelashes, the small carved nose, the jaw that was both feminine and determined.

The grandfather clock in the hallway ticked off the minutes as he studied her. It would continue to tick long after he was gone.

Steve stood up and carried her upstairs, instinctively knowing that her bedroom would be on the same side of the house as her office. It was the second door to the right, slightly ajar, her small jogging shoes overturned beside the rocking chair, her makeup brush on the dressing table, her fragrance permeating the room.

Once he could have claimed the privilege of the bed. But no more. No more.

Gently he laid her on the bed, then because it was the Moon of the Falling Leaves and she might get cold while she slept, he found a fuzzy pink afghan on the top shelf of her closet and tucked it around her.

Then he leaned over and brushed her silky hair back from her face. Softly, she stirred. Softly, she sighed.

Steve kissed her on the lips, longing to linger, longing to press his tongue between their cherry-colored folds and taste the inside of her mouth. Always so sweet. Always so warm.

"Goodbye, Angel," he whispered. "Goodbye, my love."

It was not until minutes later when the road blurred before him that Steve realized he was crying. It was the first time he'd cried since Sunny died.

Chapter Nineteen

Angel sat up, rubbing sleep from her eyes, disoriented. The pink afghan slipped from her shoulders and lay in a heap on her lap.

Steve. Steve had brought her here.

She lay back against the covers, thinking how it must have been, her curled in his arms sleeping and him bending over her bed, a big man who filled the room, a solid man who was somebody you wanted to snuggle up to once he climbed into bed.

Angel felt the hot press of tears against the back of her eyes. Steve had been in her bedroom, and she hadn't even known it.

The clock on her bedside table told her she'd slept an hour. She gave herself a pep talk.

"Well, silly goose, are you going to sit here and cry, or are you going to get ready for the banquet and the moonlight dance?"

"Angel?" It was her father's voice, calling up the stairs. "Do you think I should wear the white shirt with my tux or the pink?"

She knuckled her eyes, then went down the stairs smiling. This was her father's big evening, and she wasn't about to ruin it.

"What's Kaki wearing? Do you know?"

"Something soft and pretty...hmm, now let me see. I think it's pink. Or is it blue?"

His color was high and his eyes bright. Angel took his arm and led him into the kitchen where she poured two glasses of tea.

"Drink up while I call her." She sipped her tea while the phone rang. "Kaki? This is Angel."

"After all these years, I think I recognize your voice." *Good.* Kaki was her usual brisk self.

"Tell me what you're wearing so I can coordinate Dad's evening look."

"My dress is pink...chiffon. Carl likes soft fabric on me."

Angel smiled. Kaki and her father were going to be so good for each other. He gave her a sense of her own femininity and she gave him purpose.

Then, of course, there was love. She'd seen the way the two of them were, the secret smiles, the sparkling glances, the fingers intertwined.

"Are you nervous about tonight, Kaki?"

"No. Is Carl?"

"Right now he doesn't know his left foot from his right, but when he sees you, he'll be fine."

Kaki laughed. "I'm so happy I could dance."

"Tell Dad that."

"I already did, Angel, but I want you to know it, too. Carl Mercer has made me the happiest woman alive."

Angel was smiling when she hung up and sat down beside her dad.

"Kaki says you've made her the happiest woman alive."

"And what about you, sweetheart? Are you happy?"

"I'm happy and thrilled, Dad. I'm glad you've found someone and I'm glad it's Kaki."

"I'm not talking about us. I'm talking about you." Carl covered her hand with his own. "I've been worried about you since Thunderhorse came to Oxford. Both of us have."

"I'm fine, Dad."

"You're sure?"

"Absolutely, positively. I'm excited about my new book—I'm even thinking of moving to New York after the wedding."

He had a way of seeing right through her, so Angel got up and put her glass in the dishwasher. "You shouldn't be thinking of a thing right now except the speech you're going to make this evening when I proudly announce my father's engagement."

"My speech? I didn't know I'd have to give a speech."

He was mildly alarmed. Angel found it comical coming from the man who had stood before a classroom for twenty-five years, lecturing.

"Nothing formal, Dad. Just say whatever is in your heart."

"Well, all right, then, that's better."

The banquet had been set up in the Grove on the university campus with individual tables scattered about and a large semicircular arrangement up front for the special guests, backed by the stage that held the orchestra.

Japanese lanterns were strung from the trees, and rosebushes in pots were everywhere, giving the Grove a lush romantic look. Evening had brought considerable relief from the heat, and even the moon cooperated. It was full and spectacular, of a peculiar brightness that would be remarked upon when the revelers returned to their homes.

"Did you ever see such a moon?" they would say.

It was a moon and a night to remember.

That was what Angel was thinking as she took her seat at the center of the head table, flanked by Carl and Kaki. The president of the American Diabetes Association and his wife were already there, smiling at the prospect of so much money coming into the charity coffers. The Wild West Show tomorrow would be attended by more than a thousand people, but the moonlight dinner and dance was a special event for the donors who were really serious about giving, those who had contributed five hundred dollars or more to Angel's favorite charity.

Other dignitaries were there—the president of the university and his wife, the dean and his companion, the officers of the local chapter of the American Diabetes Association.

The only seat empty at the head table was the one reserved for Steve Thunderhorse, owner and star of the Wild West Show. Would he come? And if he did, what would she do?

Jenny Cordova and Britt Ace were at a table near the front, and they had come early because Jenny said she didn't want to miss a thing. Britt was more than willing to accommodate her. He had his own reasons for coming early. He hadn't liked the atmosphere among the media at the press conference. He sensed something of the jackal in them all, watching to see if the lion would fall, licking their lips at the prospect of circling the fallen king. Or in this case the queen, as well.

Britt wanted to keep an eye out. There was something

noble about his motives—protecting the innocent, battling the enemy—that made him expansive. He leaned toward Jenny and took her hand.

"Did I tell you how lovely you look this evening, cupcake?"

"No, you didn't. Thank you."

Her answer surprised him, but not nearly as much as her smile. God, she was a stunning woman when she wasn't trying so hard to be a witch.

"Do you think he'll be here?" He nodded toward the empty chair at the head table.

"That's what I was wondering myself. So is Angel."

"How can you tell?"

"Don't you see the way she keeps glancing at that empty chair?" Suddenly Jenny squeezed his hand. "Good Lord, would you look at that?"

Britt was not the only one swiveling to "look at that." Steve Thunderhorse cut quite a figure as he made his way to the head table in his tuxedo.

"Oh, my God," Jenny groaned.

"What's wrong? Are you sick?"

"No, but I think I'm going to be."

"I'll take you out of here."

Britt was already shoving back his chair when Jenny put a hand on his arm.

"Sit still. It's not that kind of sick. Oh, my God, just look at her face. Angel's in love with him."

Jenny was right. If ever there was love plainly written, it was the expression on Angel Mercer's face. Britt felt a quick flash of envy. After all, it didn't seem fair that Thunderhorse had succeeded where he had failed. But there was something else, too, an emotion totally foreign to Britt's selfish nature. He felt fear. Not for himself, but for a friend.

"Nothing good can come of this," he said darkly.

"You've got that right. He's already hurt her once, and from the looks of things, he's going to do it all over again."

"Not if I have anything to say about it."

"What, Britt? What can you do?"

"I can monopolize her. I can dance every dance with Angel."

Jenny was nodding and smiling her approval, which shot her up several notches in his estimation.

"I hope you don't take my defection personally," he added. Britt turned his attention back to the head table. Both Angel and Thunderhorse were trying to hide their interest, but if the secret glances they were stealing at each other were any indication, there were smoldering sparks in the Grove just waiting to burst into flame.

Chapter Twenty

Angel was grateful when the food arrived, grateful for something to do besides steal covert glances at Steve. Dean Whitaker's companion leaned over and asked about Angel's latest book, and she was even grateful for that.

"I've put Muriel in the Old West this time," she said.

"How interesting."

What had the woman said her name was? Emma? Imogene? Emily? Angel had to focus on something besides Steve or she would never get through the evening.

"And what prompted you to do that?" Emma, Imogene, Emily asked.

"My muse."

It was a stock answer to a frequently asked question. Angel figured that her smile was the only thing that saved her from sounding like a smarty-pants.

Satisfied, the woman turned back to Dean Whitaker, who

was addressing her as Marvalene. Angel would have to remember that.

Trying to be subtle and hoping she succeeded, she cas
her gaze toward Thunderhorse and found him looking righ
at her. Not merely looking, but drawing her into his glance
holding her there, a willing captive.

A delicious feeling the French so aptly called a *frissor*
stole over her, and she gave up all pretense of not staring
Let the press make something of a glance if they would
She no longer cared.

"Care for dessert, ma'am?"

Reluctantly she turned her attention toward the waiter.

"Yes, please."

Not because she was hungry, but because having a slice
of pie in front of her gave her something to toy with while
her mind wandered in the direction of the impossibly appealing Sioux. The way he looked in a tux ought to be
outlawed. He was armed and dangerous, his weapon his
brooding bronzed good looks, the danger to a woman whose
mind daily turned to flights of fancy, whether she wanted i
to or not.

That was how she might look on this fatal attraction—
completely involuntary. An irrepressible impulse. Beyond
her control.

"Angel." It was her dad, drawing her attention away
from Steve. "Your hand is cold. Are you nervous?"

"Nervous?" Was he on to her? Was she worrying her
father with all this teenage mooning and swooning? "Abou
what?"

"The band just gave the fanfare, honey. I think that'
your cue to take the microphone."

"Oh...of course."

The lighting crew put a spotlight on her when she walked
onstage. She'd deliberately worn red, a dress both bold and

passionate, a strong color to make a strong statement. Sequins, sparkly and brash. Anything except the gauzy old-fashioned dresses she preferred and Steve loved. Too many memories. Too much heartbreak.

"Ladies and gentlemen," she said. "Welcome."

Flashbulbs popped.

She didn't know what she said after that, but it must have been all right. The audience gave her a standing ovation. Angel played her role well—pause and smile, no matter what. No matter if her heart hurt or her eyes watered from all the flashbulbs or she'd had a wretched day and really wanted to do nothing but slop around in jeans and dirty tennis shoes, snarling and growling.

The welcome speech was over, the applause ended, and the audience settled back into their seats, watching her expectantly.

"As many of you know, I started this annual event ten years ago because of a courageous and wonderful man. A diabetic for twenty years, he's fought and won many battles, including diabetic retinopathy and stroke. That man is here this evening, our guest of honor, my father, Carl Mercer. Dad, would you stand?"

The applause was thunderous when he stood up. Distinguished and charming, his silver hair shining in the spotlight, he lifted a hand in salute to the gathering.

"We have double cause for celebration this evening," Angel said. "It gives me great pleasure to announce the engagement of my father, Carl Mercer, and my research assistant and trusted friend, Kaki Elliott."

The spotlight picked up a radiant Kaki, and at the calls of "Speech, speech," Angel happily relinquished the stage to them.

Carl took the microphone. "She stole my heart," he said, tears shining in his eyes.

Kaki leaned toward the mike. ''Ditto,'' she said, then gave him a sweet chaste kiss on the mouth that was both public and intensely private.

Watching from the wings, Angel brushed her own tears away. It wouldn't do to start crying. If she did she might never stop.

Amid all the applause and the hubbub of reporters taking photos and the friends rushing to the stage to offer congratulations, she signaled the band to start playing. They gave the first dance to Carl and Kaki, then people in the audience paired off and drifted toward the roped-off grassy area where Japanese lanterns cast soft shadows and October breezes stirred the branches of ancient oaks and magnolias.

They danced. Two by two. Couples. Pairs. Partners. Lovers.

That was the way it should be, Angel thought. A person was not meant to be alone.

But there she was, isolated in the midst of a crowd. Alone.

Her eyes sought and found a solitary figure on the other side of the crowd. Steve Thunderhorse, looking right back at her, eyes dark and piercing.

Would he ask her to dance? And what would she do if he did?

She wouldn't refuse him of course. That would create a spectacle, call attention, draw the press.

She would be in his arms, under the moonlight. Shivers ran through her. It would be wonderful and terrible.

''Let's dance, Angel.''

''What?'' She blinked to see Britt standing beside her.

''I said, let's dance.''

''How long have you been standing here?''

''Long enough.''

''What's that supposed to mean?''

She sounded petulant and accusatory, even to herself.

Well, fine. That was how she felt. And pretty darned mad, besides.

She was sick and tired of being the object of everybody's curiosity.

"Come on, Angel. The moon's full and the band is playing. I don't want to fight. I want to dance."

Without further ado, Britt swept her into the waltz. He was an excellent dancer, and keeping up with him required a great deal of concentration. Thank the Lord. That meant she didn't have time to keep up with Steve.

Was he dancing with another woman? Was she wearing something soft and gauzy? Something white? Who was the wretched upstart, anyhow? And did he enjoy dancing with her?

"You're stiff as a poker, Angel. Loosen up."

"I don't want to loosen up."

"Ouch. Are we feeling a little prickly tonight?"

"I'm feeling fine. Speak for yourself."

Britt executed a complicated step that she followed. More or less.

He grinned at her. "Need some practice, Angel, or are we just a bit distracted?"

"If you don't stop using that insufferable *we,* I'm going to stomp on your feet, then box your ears and storm off."

"That's good. That's *great.* Take all that hostility out on me. That's what friends are for."

She enjoyed her huffiness for about three minutes, then she felt sheepish. And ungrateful. After all, Britt was the one who had saved her from the rumor mongers at the press conference.

"I'm sorry," she said as the band segued into a sedate foxtrot.

"No problem." He stopped all the fancy stuff and just

started dancing. "I'm here to see that nobody bothers you tonight. And I mean *nobody*."

She nodded. That was fine with her. Or was it?

Suddenly *nobody* danced by with a presumptuous hussy who had her gall. Steve turned and Angel saw that it was neither a presumptuous hussy nor a wretched upstart, but her best friend Jenny. Jenny winked at her.

"Are you two in cahoots?" Angel said to Britt.

"I'll never tell," he said, swinging her into the tango as the band switched to a hot Latin beat.

Steve would have given his right arm to know what Britt Ace and Angel were talking about. He didn't trust the man. He was too smooth, too cunning, too handsome. What was he smiling about? Was he flirting with Angel? Winning her back?

He missed a beat, stepped on Jenny's foot. "Sorry," he muttered. Music wasn't his strong suit, neither dancing nor singing. And certainly not guitar playing.

"No problem," she said.

What was he doing on the dance floor, anyhow?

It didn't take a genius to answer that question. Angel had danced every dance with Britt Ace, and the only way Steve could keep up with her was to stay on the floor.

Poor Jenny. She was looking a little frazzled around the edges, and no wonder. He guessed he'd stepped on her toes half a dozen times.

"Why don't we sit this one out?" she said. "I'm not very good at these Latin tunes."

He escorted her back to her table. "Thanks for the dances," he said.

"You're welcome."

She had the pursed-lip look of a woman who was going

to say, "Sit down, stay and chat a while." Steve left quickly before he got trapped.

Not that Jenny Cordova was bad company. In fact, talking to her would be interesting, particularly if she mentioned Angel, even in passing.

But he would never be able to keep up with Angel if he stayed at the table. He strolled through the area in the general direction of the bar. But a drink was the last thing on his mind. He'd spotted Angel, still dancing with Britt.

Steve wanted to throttle him. Ramming his fists into his pockets, he leaned against the trunk of a giant magnolia, which gave him both protection from the crowd and a panoramic view of the dance floor.

The Japanese lanterns swung in the light breeze that had sprung up, and an occasional flashbulb lit the night as reporters roved the crowd looking for stories. Most of the activity centered around Angel.

She was good with the press. Steve watched as she paused, posed, smiled, then resumed dancing as if nothing had happened. Camera-ready at all times, Britt Ace was eating it up.

Steve squelched the urge to snatch Angel out of Britt's arms and steal away into the night. His emotions were getting out of hand. He knew that.

"I should leave," he muttered.

Suddenly there was a whirlwind of activity around Angel; flashbulbs exploded, reporters circled, insistent and invasive.

Damn the consequences, Steve thought as he headed her way.

"You and Britt Ace have been cozy all evening," one of them said.

"We haven't been cozy," Angel said. "We're dancing."

The reporter was persistent. "But you and he were once engaged?"

"Yes."

"Does this mean you've resumed your engagement?"

"No," Angel said. "He's a friend. Nothing more."

"Gentlemen, please." Britt held up his hand, laughing.

"Believe me, the man who claims Miss Mercer's affection will be lucky, indeed. I'd like nothing more than to be that man. I'm not. We're dancing, that's all." The self-deprecating laughter again. "And you're in our way."

Britt tried to maneuver her once more into a dance, but the reporters surrounded them, firing question, taking pictures. Steve wanted to rush in, grab Angel and take her out of there, but that would only increase the feeding frenzy.

Instead, he strolled quietly into their midst, passing unnoticed until he had planted himself solidly between Angel and her nemesis.

"Gentlemen, I believe I'm the one you've been looking for," he said.

"Thunderhorse!" one of them yelled, and in the general melee that followed, Steve turned quietly to Britt.

"Take her out of here," he said, then blocked for them as they left the dance floor.

When he turned back to the reporters, he was smiling. Nobody noticed that he was as tightly coiled as a cobra, his eyes dark and predatory, his smile as icy and unwelcoming as one of the unusual ice storms that sometimes paralyzed the South.

"Now, gentlemen, what can I do for you?"

Angel was numb. As Britt led her away, she felt like a kitten who had been flattened by a steamroller.

Glancing back over her shoulder, she saw Thunderhorse facing the reporters. He looked like a mountain, immovable and everlasting.

Jenny jumped up from her table when she saw them coming. Britt took her hand.

"Jenny, find out what the Sioux warrior is up to, then follow us to the conservatory."

"You want me to get in the middle of that fray?"

"Close enough to snoop, and don't argue."

Everything looked blurry around the edges to Angel. Even Jenny, last seen standing by her table, military-fashion, saluting.

"That Jenny's a card," Britt said.

Angel didn't answer. Nothing seemed to be required of her this evening but to be led around like a calf going to the slaughter.

Britt hurried them underneath the Japanese lanterns, past the bandstand, through the magnolia trees. He was striding past the parking lot when she dug in her heels.

"Stop."

"Are you cold?"

Britt pulled off his tuxedo jacket and draped it over her shoulders.

"No, I am not cold."

"Mad, then? Good. That's better than scared. Keep walking, Angel."

She dug in her heels again. "This is ridiculous. Where are you taking me?"

"Out of that madhouse. This new breed of reporter is a royal pain in the association. I'm glad I'm from the old school."

As much as she hated to admit it, Britt's chatter made Angel feel better. Almost human.

"Slow down, Britt. You're walking too fast. Can we sit down and rest awhile?"

"Sure thing." He led her to a park bench underneath a

chinaberry tree. "You don't see many trees like this anymore. This one has character."

"I'm so tired of being in a fishbowl," Angel said, ignoring the conversational gambit about trees. "I'm nobody special. Why can't they let me be normal?"

"Because the public has a rapacious appetite for scandal, my dear, especially if it involves the rich and famous. These days, any journalist looking to capture a headline is going to dig for dirt and sensationalism."

"I wish they'd stop digging in my backyard."

Angel thought of Arizona with its broad blue skies where eagles soared, its solid walls of rock carved by time, its cool green rivers where a solitary fisherman could sit on the bank and cast his pole in peace. She thought of quiet mornings on Paradise Ranch, of standing at the kitchen window barefoot looking at the horses racing around the paddocks, tails flying like the flags of small countries.

And thinking of those things, she longed.

Jenny hurried into view. "Good grief, what a scene."

"What's happening back there?" Britt asked.

"They're firing cannons at him, and he's catching the balls with his bare hands. First he shamed them, said they were abusing Angel's hospitality, turning the benefit into a media circus, then he stonewalled." Jenny laughed. "I think I'm beginning to like that man."

"Same here." Britt propped his foot on the bench beside Angel. "He rescued a bad situation that I created."

"Don't be so hard on yourself," Jenny said.

"I should have guessed what would happen when I monopolized Angel."

Jenny put her hand on his arm. "You couldn't have known."

Angel was torn between anger and fascination, anger that Britt had manipulated her and fascination at the exchange between her two friends. She'd thought they hated each other.

"What's going on here?" she said.

"Good intentions gone awry." Britt looked sheepish, a first for him. "All I meant to do was keep you occupied for the evening, and safe."

"Safe? From reporters? Sometimes they get overly enthusiastic, but I've never felt that I'm in danger."

"Not from them, honey," Jenny said. "From Thunderhorse. Though I have to admit he's not as bad as I thought. He can't dance worth a hoot, but he has manners, which is more than I can say for some people." She looked pointedly at Britt.

"Now, cupcake…"

Angel stood up and put her arms around their shoulders. "Now, listen, you two. The band will be playing the last song in a little while, and you haven't even danced together. Go back and enjoy yourselves."

"Are you kidding?" This was from Jenny. "And leave you out here for the wolves?"

"You're forgetting something, Jenny. This is my hometown. I'm as safe here as I was in the cradle. Besides, I'm through running away." She gave them a little shove. "Go on. I'll join you in a minute. I'm not going to miss Dad and Kaki's big evening just because the two of you think I can't take care of myself."

"No way," Britt said. "I escorted you out of there, I'll escort you back."

"Britt, the only thing bigger than your mouth is your ego." Jenny grabbed his arm. "Come one. I want to rumba."

They walked off arm in arm, and Britt's voice drifted back to Angel. "I've never heard it called that before."

"Shut up, Britt, before I change my mind about you."

He'd forgotten his coat. Angel pulled it around her shoulders, then leaned back and closed her eyes. It was peaceful out here all by herself with nothing but the song of cicadas and crickets to mar the silence.

She would sit a while longer, then put in a brief appearance at the dance and go home to bed. These past few days had sapped her energy.

"Hello, Angel."

Steve's voice washed over her like warm honey, and Angel sat with her eyes closed a moment longer, afraid that when she opened them she might discover she was only dreaming.

The body heat she felt when he sat down beside her was no dream. She looked at him, tall and chiseled and fine in the moonlight.

"How did you find me?"

"I'm Sioux," he said, as if that explained everything.

And she guessed it did. Even his stubborn pride that kept them apart.

A great stillness descended on them, and she sat beside him yearning. Did he know? Did he care? Would a man who cared nothing for a woman take the time to cover her with a pink afghan?

"I should go back," she said.

Steve didn't argue as she'd thought he might. Instead he tucked her hand into the crook of his arm.

"I'll walk back with you."

She might have said "No." She might have said, "The reporters will be watching." She might have said, "We have nothing more to say to each other, to do with each other."

But she didn't. She walked beside him, loving the way her head barely came to his shoulder, loving the feel of his arm underneath her hand, loving the way the moon made a silver path for them to walk upon.

In the distance the band was playing a song that was vaguely familiar. She remembered the tune but not the words, and so she hummed along. It was that kind of song.

"Your voice is lovely," Steve said.

"Thank you."

"Did you save the last dance for me, Angel?"

It was his way of saying, "I don't care what the reporters make of us. I don't care if they snap pictures. I don't care about anything except holding you in my arms, just once, just this once."

Wasn't that what he was saying? Or was it her vivid imagination?

"Yes," she said. "I saved the last dance for you."

I will always save the last dance for you.

The light from the Japanese lanterns cut through the darkness, and the hum of the crowd drowned out the sound of cicadas. Soon they would be surrounded by people. Soon they would lose this precious moment of privacy.

There was so much she wanted to say, so much she needed to say. And so little time to say it.

"Steve..."

"Yes?"

He looked down at her, handsome, attentive, but still so careful. One look at his shuttered eyes, his closed masklike expression, and Angel completely changed her mind. There was nothing she could say that would alter their situation.

"Thank you coming to make this benefit a success."

"You're welcome."

As they walked onto the dance floor, the Japanese lanterns shot sparks off her dress, and the last strains of the song faded.

The conductor stepped up to the microphone amidst applause. "Good night, ladies and gentlemen. Thank you for coming."

"It looks as if we missed our dance," Steve said.

She hid her disappointment behind a brave smile. At least it felt brave to her.

"It wouldn't have been the same without the horse," she said.

Was that a tiny crack showing in his facade? Did her remark hit some tender spot reserved just for her?

Angel didn't stick around to see.

"Good night, Steve," she said, then, head held high, she walked away.

Chapter Twenty-One

Steve let her go. It was the decent thing to do, the noble thing. Standing under the Japanese lanterns, he watched her go to her father and Kaki, watched her smile and put her arms around them.

He wasn't the only one watching her. Everybody who came within radius watched Angel and was charmed.

Is this a spell I'm under? Steve wondered. Or am I in love? For the first time in my life? Really in love? Forever?

The crowd began to disperse and he saw Angel leave.

Look back, he silently pleaded. Look back at me, just once.

As if she'd heard him, her steps slowed, then stopped altogether. She turned, and he saw her searching for him across the meandering crowd.

I'm here, Angel. I'm here.

Moonlight shimmered in her hair, red roses flanked her

and, seeing him, she smiled. He would always remember her that way.

And he knew. He was in love. Forever.

He held the moment close, not moving until she broke contact. Then she disappeared into the darkness, and he went back to his room to wrestle with demons.

Angel and Thunderhorse were in the news again.

Sitting in her office with copies of the local paper, as well as four others spread around her, Angel scanned the headlines: SIOUX STANDOFF and ANGEL MERCER ANNOUNCES FATHER'S ENGAGEMENT, from Atlanta; LOVE IN THE AIR, with photos of Carl, Kaki and Angel side by side with a photo of Steve Thunderhorse, from Memphis; BENEFIT TAKES BACK SEAT TO LOVE, with photos of Carl and Kaki beside the photo of Thunderhorse and Angel in Arizona, from New Orleans.

Angel picked up the paper from New Orleans and started reading. "In Oxford, Mississippi, where magnolias spread their massive branches and Japanese lanterns cast soft shadows in the perfumed night, the benefit dinner and dance for the American Diabetes Association took a back seat last night to love.

"Bestselling novelist Angel Mercer announced the engagement of her father, retired history professor Carl Mercer, to her longtime secretary/research assistant Kaki Elliott. But it was not the senior Mercer whose love took the spotlight. It was none other than Steve Thunderhorse."

Angel groaned. Would the media never let go?

She read on. "Once again, Thunderhorse rode to Angel's rescue, this time on the dance floor where journalists surrounded her, firing questions and flashbulbs."

The next few paragraphs told how Steve had come between her and the press and how she had escaped with Britt Ace, her former fiancé.

Angel picked up her coffee cup and took a fortifying gulp. "That was years ago," she fumed to herself. "Don't they ever forget a thing?"

The article continued, "After thoroughly excoriating the press for hounding Miss Mercer and turning the benefit into a media circus, Steve Thunderhorse stonewalled. When asked if he had come to Oxford to see Miss Mercer, he gave a terse, 'No comment.' When asked if his visit was personal, as well as professional, his reply was again, 'No comment.'

"Good for you, Steve," Angel said. "You show them."

The newspaper threatened to slide off her desk, and she slapped it back into place. It felt good to hit something.

"To questions about his past, his ex-wife, his daughter, his career, the stony-faced Sioux still responded, 'No comment.'

Stony-faced was not the description Angel would use for Thunderhorse. Never. Carved granite, perhaps. A statue cast in bronze. Noble. Magnificent. Delicious.

She read on. "There was only one question that got a response from Steve Thunderhorse. When asked if he loved Angel Mercer, he replied, 'Love is not for public record.'"

Angel's breath snagged in her throat, and she read Steve's statement again.

Love is not for public record.

Her hand trembled as she set the newspaper aside. A stream of sunlight from the window illuminated the statement, gave it import, dignity.

Love is not for public record. Steve hadn't denied love.

"He loves me," she whispered. "Steve Thunderhorse loves me."

Thousands had come to see the Wild West Show. Standing in the wings with Wayne, Steve scanned the crowd for

Angel. She was not there. The box seats reserved for family were filled with Kaki, Carl, Jenny and Britt.

Where was Angel?

"Looks like we drew a crowd," Wayne said.

"Yes."

"I'm glad. I always enjoy doing the show for a good cause."

"Yes."

Steve continued his search. What if Angel was sick? What if she had gone?

"Steve." Wayne's hand was on his shoulder. "Is anything wrong?"

"No." Everything was wrong. *He* was wrong. He'd been wrong from the very beginning. He'd been wrong to leave Emily, wrong to leave her in her condition. He'd been wrong to leave Angel. Wrong not to tell her he loved her.

He loved her. Still, he marveled at the miracle. He loved Angel Mercer.

And yet he could do nothing about it. Not yet. Not until he'd straightened out the mess he'd left behind.

"Thanks for asking, Wayne," he said.

"You bet. Anytime."

The band began to tune up. Today they would have live music for the show, and Wayne would be working the lighting and sound.

"It's about that time." Wayne headed toward the control booth, then called back over his shoulder. "Break a leg, Steve."

Steve didn't reply, for suddenly there was Angel. Just as the band started its fanfare, she appeared at the doorway, dressed in white, her hair long and flowing, her hat with a pink ribbon dangling from her hand. It was the dress he loved, the old-fashioned look he loved, the woman he loved.

"Did you wear the dress for me?" he whispered, and he knew in his heart that she had.

As she moved toward her place in the box seat, front and center, Steve whistled softly for Shadow. The white stallion tossed his mane, then proudly carried his rider into the spotlight.

To thunderous applause, Shadow pranced, two-stepped and danced his way into the hearts of the audience. But Steve had only one heart in mind.

He waved his hat to the crowd in general, but his eyes were on one woman. Angel had made it to her reserved box and stood in front of her seat watching him, smiling at him.

So much in a glance. So much in a smile.

The crowd receded as they stared at each other. Did time stand still or did it only seem that way?

I love you, Angel, his heart whispered. Did she hear? Did she know?

The band leader lifted his baton, cymbals crashed, drums rolled, and the fanfare came to a halt, leaving Steve and Angel alone in the spotlight.

The crowd waited, watched, breathless. Steve gave a signal, and Shadow took a deep bow toward Angel's box, paying homage to the queen. Angel unwound the ribbon from her hat and then moved slowly toward Steve.

They met at the railing.

"You are so beautiful," he murmured. *I love you.*

"Thank you," she whispered. *I love you.*

Then, leaning down, she handed him the ribbon. Never taking his eyes from hers, Steve tied the ribbon around his sleeve, an ancient knight riding into battle wearing his lady's colors.

The crowd was on its feet, applauding wildly. Angel took her seat, and Steve took center ring.

It was time for the show to begin.

Angel watched the spotlight follow Thunderhorse to the center ring.

"Ladies and gentlemen, thank you for coming to the tenth annual Oxford Diabetes Benefit," he said. "I am Thunderhorse and this is my companion, Shadow. In support of this worthwhile cause, I'm happy to present to you the one hundredth—and final—Wild West Show."

Thunderhorse went immediately into his Sitting Bull routine, but Angel hardly heard a thing he said. His final show? Why? Did that mean he was leaving Arizona? Leaving Paradise Ranch? Going back into photojournalism? Going back to D.C.?

Jenny leaned over to whisper, "This guy is good."

"He's better than good," Britt said. "He's great. Wish I'd known about him before he decided to give it all up. I might still do a feature on him. You know, Pulitzer prize–winner goes back to his roots."

"Shush," Jenny said. "Watch the show."

Onstage Thunderhorse was telling the story of the massacre at Wounded Knee. Angel leaned forward, riveted. He had not told that story in Arizona. She supposed he changed shows often.

Standing in the spotlight, his rich voice rising and falling over his rapt audience, Thunderhorse made the pain of his people come alive. As he told of bodies strewn across the snow, he brought the chill of winter into the arena. When he told of the sagging banner in the Episcopal church where the survivors lay, the banner that said Peace on Earth, Good Will to Men, he brought tears to their eyes. And when he quoted the Sioux chieftain's speech about the hoop of a nation being broken and the death of dreams, a few wept openly.

"Here." Britt pulled his handkerchief out of his pocket and handed it to Angel. She wiped her face, then passed it to Jenny. Out of the corner of her eye she saw Kaki and her father both surreptitiously wiping their eyes.

"This is the best show we've ever had," Carl said.

"I agree," Kaki said. "Too bad it's his last."

Thunderhorse received a standing ovation.

"Because this show has been built around the life and times of my ancestor, Sitting Bull," Thunderhorse said when the applause let up, "and because this is my final show, I'm going to re-create his death—after the intermission."

As the spotlight faded, Angel's companions burst into animated chatter, but she sat perfectly still, straining for one last glimpse of Thunderhorse.

"Do you want some…Angel? Angel?" Jenny touched her hand. "Are you all right, kiddo?"

"I'm fine. Just a little ragged around the edges."

"That's a yes," Jenny told Britt, and he hurried off toward the concession stand.

"What did I say yes to?"

"Lemonade." When Carl and Kaki had gone for refreshments, Jenny leaned back in her seat. "Now, tell Mother Jenny about that pink ribbon."

Angel had always been open with Jenny. There was no need to hide the truth now.

"I wanted to leave a part of me with him."

The usually voluble Jenny was quiet for a long time. Then she squeezed Angel's hand.

"There's a really great apartment across from Central Park that would work well for you, I think. Lots of light, lots of open space."

"I'll think about it."

"Seriously?"

"Yes, seriously."

Britt returned with lemonade, the lights went down and

the show began. Dressed as Sitting Bull, Thunderhorse re-created the events that led to his death. When the bullet rang out that brought him to the ground, the band struck up a slow funereal song, and Shadow began to dance. Riderless. The Dance of the Ghosts, Thunderhorse had called it, and it was the last dance the stallion would do.

There would be no romantic ballads, no invitation to Angel to lean back in the arms of the man she loved while the band played "Embraceable You," no riding off into the sunset.

The spotlight on the fallen Sioux faded to a pinpoint of light. And then suddenly, darkness.

"It's over," Jenny said, not talking about the show at all.

But Angel refused to believe that, for in the brief instant before the stage went dark, she'd seen a tiny glint of pink.

Steve Thunderhorse still wore her colors.

Chapter Twenty-Two

After the show well-wishers from the audience swarmed around Steve. Even Britt, who was completely won over.

"I'm going down to see if I can corner him about doing a TV special," he'd said.

Afterward, Jenny laughed. "He's just like any little kid at a Wild West Show. He wants to pet the horse."

"I want to pet the horse, too," Carl said, and everybody laughed.

"Angel," Kaki said, "we're going down to thank Thunderhorse for a magnificent performance and see if there are any last-minute details he needs help with. Or do you want to take care of that personally?"

Angel studied the man in the arena—handsome, self-assured, talented, wounded. An old adage came into her mind: If you love something, let it go and it will come back to you.

She was letting go. If Steve loved her, he would come back.

"No," she told Kaki. "You go ahead. I think I'll go back home and work on the book." She forced a smile for Kaki and her dad's sake. "My muse is calling."

Jenny took Angel's elbow and hustled her out.

"Wait a minute." Angel's protest was not very strong. "What do you think you're doing?"

"Getting you out of here before you cry."

"I'm not going to cry."

"You should see the look on your face."

By the time they got to the parking lot, Angel was already crying. Jenny got behind the wheel of Angel's car and drove her home.

"What about Britt?" Angel said.

"He can take care of himself." Turning into the driveway, Jenny sideswiped a forsythia bush.

"Careful, that's my car."

"You won't be needing it in New York."

"How do you know I'm going to New York?"

"Because Carl and Kaki are going to need some time alone so they can adjust to being married."

"They're not married yet," Angel said as they climbed the front porch steps.

"A minor detail," Jenny said, brushing that aside. "And in the second place, you don't need to be sitting on the sidelines watching somebody else in love."

"That somebody else happens to be my father."

"Even more the reason you don't need to be on the sidelines."

Jenny barreled into the kitchen and began making hot tea while Angel perched on a bar stool, morose.

"You're doing that all wrong."

"Are you trying to tell a Yankee how to make tea? Shame on you."

The tea was bracing and delicious, and Angel had the grace to tell Jenny so.

"Now, tell me about this book you're working on. I'm dying to know."

"Muriel falls in love."

Jenny cocked her head to one side, pondering. "I like it," she said.

As always, when Angel talked about a story, everything else in her life receded into the background and her characters took over. The more she talked, the more excited she became.

"This book is writing itself," she said, and Jenny laughed.

"You say that about all your books. That's why you're so good, kiddo." Jenny poured two more cups of tea. "Feeling better?"

"Yes. Thanks, Jenny."

"You can thank me by writing another bestseller."

The last thing Steve packed was the pink ribbon, the only thing he had left of Angel Mercer. Slowly he untied the bit of satin and lifted it to his lips. The fragrance of roses wafted over him, and he closed his eyes a moment, wishing and dreaming.

Wayne knocked on the door. "We're all set to load Shadow, Steve."

"Coming."

Steve started toward his suitcase with the ribbon, but at the last minute he changed his mind and stuffed it into his shirt pocket, right over his heart.

Then he joined Wayne, and together they loaded Shadow into his special van for the long journey home.

* * *

Autumn held full sway over Paradise Ranch with golden leaves drifting in the breezes, the sweet smells of hay stored for the winter filling the barn, and the horses frisking around the paddocks enjoying the cooler weather.

Steve sat behind the desk in his office, tension knotting his neck and shoulders, while Lucas was kicked back in a cane chair chewing the end of a pencil.

"That's a bad habit, Lucas. You're going to break your teeth."

"I'm doing it in sympathy for you. What's this all about, Steve? Ever since you got back from Mississippi, you've been like a cat in a room full of rockers."

"I've decided to go back to D.C."

Lucas's pencil rolled out of his hand. "You're what? What kind of damn-fool notion is that? And who's going to run the ranch? As you may recall, this is the time of year I always go riding off into the sunset."

"Hold your horses, Lucas. I didn't make myself clear. I'm not leaving the ranch. I'm going to D.C. to bring Emily back."

"What am I missing here? The last time I looked you were over the moon for Angel."

"I still am. I love Angel. I think she's the only woman I ever loved. Including Emily."

"This is about what happened nine years ago, isn't it."

"Yes. Emily's still in a bad way. I'm partially responsible for that...." He held up his hand to stop Lucas's protest. "I know I can't take full blame. But what I can do is try and help her."

"That's decent and noble of you, but what if she doesn't want your help? And what about Angel? What do you think she's going to do while you're holed up out here with Emily?"

"Then it's all right with you if I bring her out here?"

"You don't need my permission, you know that. But yes, I can see how you need to try and straighten out the past before you move on." His eyes were lasers, piercing Steve. "You didn't answer my question. Did you tell Angel you love her? Did you ask her to wait for you?"

"No to both. It wouldn't have been fair to ask her to wait. She's young and beautiful and desirable—"

"And in love with you. I think you should tell her what you're doing, Steve."

"I've made up my mind."

"All right then. I won't try to change it." Lucas stood up and put his hand on Steve's shoulder. "Good luck, pal. I have a feeling you're going to need it."

"Good luck to you, too. Don't take any wooden nickels out there in… Where are you going, Lucas?"

"Who knows? Whichever way the wind blows. I'll leave as soon as you get back, with or without Emily."

"*With* her."

Emily still lived at their old Georgetown address.

Steve had found out through friends in D.C. As the cab turned onto the street where he'd lived, memories swamped him—Sunny in the backyard, Sunny in the kitchen eating gingerbread boys, Sunny in her room with a makeshift veil over her head.

"Daddy, can I climb a tree?"

"Daddy, can I eat all the heads?"

"Daddy, can I be a bride someday?"

Sunny would never climb another tree, never eat another gingerbread boy, never grow up to be a bride, but Steve was astonished that the memories tumbled gently through his mind, their sharp edges worn away by time.

"Here you are, sir." The cabdriver pulled over to the curb and Steve paid his fare. "You want me to wait?"

"No, thanks."

What he had to do was going to take longer than a few minutes. In fact, he didn't even know if Emily would be home. He hadn't called ahead, knowing that she would tell him no. Or hang up on him.

Steve walked up the steps and rang the doorbell. The woman who answered the door was a stranger.

"I'm looking for Emily Thunderhorse."

"Miss Emily is out. May I tell her who stopped by?"

"I'm Steve Thunderhorse."

"I'll tell her you were here."

The woman started to shut the door, but Steve stuck his foot in the way.

"I'll wait for her here, if you don't mind."

For a moment he thought the housekeeper would say no, but she didn't. His editor used to say to him, "All right. Have it your way. When you wear that I'm-taking-scalps look, I know better than to argue with you."

"I'll show you to the sitting room," she said stiffly.

"I know the way."

Emily had changed the house very little in nine years, with one notable exception. She'd ripped out the bookcases and put in a bar. Some of the upholstered furniture was looking a little shabby, which was more a testament to Emily's state of mind than her state of finances. He still paid her a substantial alimony, and she had money of her own, inherited from a grandfather who'd owned a chain of fried-chicken restaurants scattered throughout the Southeast.

Steve put his bag down and took a chair beside the window. The housekeeper didn't offer him anything to drink and he didn't ask. He was not there for comfort.

It was two hours before another cab pulled up outside.

Standing at the window, Steve saw Emily stumble out, then fumble in her purse for fare, dropping money all over the sidewalk. The driver offered to help her, but she shook off his arm, picked up the money and made her unsteady way to the front door.

The housekeeper rushed to let her in, talking to her all the while in a low-voiced murmur. There was the sound of the door slamming as the housekeeper left, then Emily stood in the doorway to the sitting room, tilted to the left, hanging on to the frame for balance.

"What are you doing here?"

Her voice was slurred from too much drink and deeper than he remembered. Nine years on the bottle had given her a whiskey voice. It had also destroyed her skin and dulled her hair. Emily looked twenty years older than when he'd last seen her.

"I came to help you, Emily."

"Help me? *Help me!*" Her laughter was bitter. "That's rich. The man who got the hell out of Dodge nine years ago is back to *help*."

"I should have stayed then. I'm sorry, Emily."

"Too little, too late, Stevie old chap. *Miss* Emily Thunderhorse has other fish to fry."

She lurched toward the bar and began to fix herself a drink.

"Can I interest you in a little libation, or has Miss Angel Mercer got you walking the straight and narrow?"

"Leave her out of this."

"Aha. Touched a nerve. Didn't know you had any." Emily lifted her glass. "Cheers, Stevie-O, down the hatch and all that jazz."

She drained her glass, then reached for the bottle again. It would be useless to try to stop her. She was already drunk, and Steve knew from experience that it was futile to argue with a drunk.

Emily glanced at Steve, her hand wavering as she poured her drink. Suddenly the bottle slipped from her hand, and she collapsed on the floor, sobbing.

Steve picked her up and carried her upstairs. Then, as tenderly as if she were a baby, he put his ex-wife to bed.

Emily grabbed his hand. "Don't leave me, Stevie."

"I'm just going to the bathroom to get a cool cloth for your head."

When he got back Emily was asleep. Sitting on the edge of the bed, Steve smoothed her tangled hair back from her puffy face.

"I'm going to help you, Emily. I promise you."

Chapter Twenty-Three

"This is the best thing you've ever done, Angel. I cried my eyes out when I read it." Over the phone Jenny's voice was still scratchy with tears.

Angel could picture her tilted back in her chair with a view of Forty-second Street on her left and her favorite Salvador Dali print on her right.

"You liked it, then?"

"*Liked* it? I loved it! I just about died when Muriel decided to become human for the sake of love and then ended up at Wounded Knee."

"I cried when I wrote that scene."

"I thought for sure they were both going to die in the massacre, then Muriel would be an angel once more, plus you'd have that gorgeous hunky Sioux all set to do sequels as her celestial lover."

"There will be no sequels."

"What are you talking about, no sequels?" Jenny was

yelling so loudly Angel had to hold the phone away from her ear. "Of *course* there'll be sequels. Writing Muriel stories is what you do."

"Muriel is no longer an angel, remember? She's now a happily married woman, raising babies with Black Hawk."

There was dead silence from Jenny's end of the line. Angel held on, waiting for the lecture she knew was coming.

"Angel, how long has it been since you last saw Thunderhorse?"

"Two months."

"And in all that time have you heard from him?"

"I know what you're thinking."

"What? What am I thinking?"

"That I'm projecting on paper that *Muriel at Wounded Knee* is my attempt to write a happy ending for myself—and that it's all fantasy."

"I don't mean to be cruel, Angel, just realistic. Thunderhorse is gone. Kaput. Split. Out of the picture."

"I know that in my mind, Jenny, but not in my heart."

"I'm sorry, kiddo. Listen, I'm sending this manuscript right over to your editor by courier, and we're not going to talk about a sequel for a while. All right? We're not even going to *think* about it."

"Great, because *no* is my final word, and I'm not going to change my mind."

"How're the wedding plans coming along?"

"You know Kaki. Efficiency is her middle name. She won't let me do a thing."

"Great. Come up here, and you'll kill two birds with one stone. You'll be out of her hair and you can rescue me from having Thanksgiving dinner in a can."

"I'll think about it."

"We can Christmas shop, look at apartments. We can watch the parade in person."

"That's not fair." Jenny knew how much she loved parades.

"When have I ever played fair? Say yes, kiddo."

"I'll *think* about it, and that's all I promise."

Chapter Twenty-Four

Sometimes memories of Angel were so sharp, so clear, Steve felt as if she was in the room with him. Tonight was one of those times, tonight with the new moon making a golden pool on his sheets.

He'd licked her skin where the moon turned it gold.

Groaning, Steve balled his hands into fists and lay stiffly in his bed, trying to control his memories, his body, his heart.

It was useless. In the bedroom down the hall Emily lay sleeping while the woman he desired more than life itself was somewhere in Mississippi believing he'd abandoned her.

Did she think of him still? Did she remember?

The pink ribbon was all he had of her. A tiny satin sliver, frayed around the edges from being switched from pocket to pocket, carried always over his heart.

Steve stole from his bed and got the tiny strip of pink out

of his shirt pocket. Putting it to his face, he inhaled deeply. The ribbon had long ago lost its scent, but Steve imagined the fragrance of roses still, old-fashioned damask roses.

He lay upon the sheets, the ribbon pressed to his lips, soft and sensual. Naked and unashamed he trailed the ribbon over his face, across his chest, down the flat planes of his belly. Satin caressed his skin, sending sensations through his body that made sleep impossible.

Groaning, he held the ribbon flat against his heart, willing Angel to think of him, to want him, to love him. With his mind he reached for her, conjured her up, brought her to his bed, lush and inviting, her skin satin against his, silky as the ribbon that made a slash of pink against the dark V of chest hair.

Her hands were on him, incredible, magical, doing things that made him moan. Her voice was in the wind whispering against his window, whispering the sweet hot erotica she sometimes used in the dark when the moon gilded the sheets and Steve covered her body.

Need was a stallion, riding him hard, and sweat slicked his body, a heated sheen, warm and wet. Angel was warm and wet, waiting for him, wanting him, wild for him, as wild as the beast that clawed at him in the lonely night.

A dark cloud moved across the moon, and lightning split the night sky. Thunder rolled close by, threatening one of the sudden storms that sometimes boiled out of the canyons.

His own tumult matched the tumult of the elements. With Angel in his heart and mind, he matched the building fury of the storm. Release came with the torrents that slashed against the window.

"Angel!" Steve cried, then lay back against the damp pillows with her satin ribbon pressed to his lips.

Angel awakened with a start.

Clutching the sheets to her chest, she sat very still, listening. A storm had come up in the night, with all the sound effects. Fat drops of rain pummeled her window like baseballs, showing a fury unlike any she'd seen in a long time.

She got out of bed and tiptoed to her dad's room. Pushing open the door, she peeped in. He was sleeping soundly, his chest rising and falling under the mound of quilts.

Shivering, Angel hurried back to her own room, but she couldn't sleep. She was filled with a restless need, a restless longing.

Crossing to the window, she pressed her face against the cool pane. The force of the storm was so great she could almost feel the rain pelting her face like blows to her sensitive skin.

Something deep and urgent tugged at her again, and suddenly she knew. Shivers shook her, but not from the cold, not at all from the cold.

"Steve," she cried, her knees weak and her heart hurting.

Chapter Twenty-Five

The Thanksgiving wreath on the door of Steve's house at Paradise Ranch was not much, just cheap imitation pine boughs with artificial turkeys and a plastic pilgrim attached, but it was one of the prettiest sights Steve had ever seen. Not because of what it was, but because of who had put it there.

It was not merely a wreath, but a symbol of recovery. The road back had been long, the battle fought hard and sometimes bitter, but finally she'd made it. Steve admired the wreath a while longer, then opened the front door and called out her name.

"Emily."

She came down the stairs, wraith thin, her hair still dull and listless but clean and brushed into a careful pageboy. Best of all, she was smiling.

"I like the wreath," he said.

She laughed. "I wanted to do something to show my appreciation."

"You didn't have to go overboard," he said, teasing her. The easy camaraderie felt good.

"I didn't. I put it on your bill."

She'd reached the bottom of the staircase, and he took both her hands.

"I'm so proud of you, Emily."

"I could never have done it without you, Steve." She squeezed his hands. "I mean that. I've been in and out of clinics for years, but nobody *cared* the way you do."

"I care, Emily." He sniffed. "Mmm, something smells—"

"Burned," she said. "I burned dinner again."

Still holding her hand, Steve headed to the kitchen. "Looks like we're in for another meal of my famous cowboy stew."

In the kitchen Emily perched on a bar stool while Steve gathered ingredients.

"It's just my luck to always fall for women who can't cook. Angel..."

Guiltily, he shot his ex-wife a glance.

"It's all right, Steve. You don't have to avoid saying her name. I know you still love her."

Steve wasn't about to get into a discussion of Angel with Emily. Not that he doubted her sincerity. She had made a complete turnaround, emotionally, as well as physically.

She'd said caring was the key, and he supposed that was true. Certainly it had been true in his case. But the place itself was a powerful healing element. Isolated and peaceful, it was also spectacularly beautiful in a way that left no doubt that someone greater was in charge, that man was a mere grain of sand, a blip on the screen of time, an insignificant being given custody of the land for a short while.

"I've been thinking about ways to repay your kindness, Steve."

"I need no repayment."

"I knew you'd say that, but nevertheless, I want to do something, make some grand gesture before I go...."

"You don't have to go. I want you to be secure in the knowledge that you've licked this thing before you leave Paradise Ranch."

"How can I know, Steve? How can I ever know what I'm capable of doing as long as I'm here, coddled and wrapped in cotton wool?" She wrapped her arms around herself, shivering.

"Cold?"

"Yes. Suddenly."

Steve got a warm jacket from the peg beside the kitchen door and handed it to her. She watched silently while he got the stew cooking.

"Do you remember what our favorite thing used to be this time of year?" she said.

"Yes."

Steve wasn't in the mood for a trip down memory lane. There was something in him pushing for release, something hungry, something urgent. And it had nothing to do with the woman in his kitchen.

"Good, because I decided that my last gesture before returning to Georgetown will be to re-create Thanksgiving past." She smiled, triumphant. "I've made reservations and booked us into the Algonquin—you needn't look so alarmed. I booked separate rooms. We'll arrive just in time for Macy's Thanksgiving Day Parade."

Emily had booked them into the Dorothy Parker suite.

"Two rooms," she said after they arrived. "Only not

separate," she confessed. "Beats all that running between doors to coordinate our plans."

Steve didn't argue. He hated controversy and contention, and besides, he didn't want to do anything to spoil Emily's trip. This was her big celebration, and he was determined to make the best of it.

It was not what he had planned, however. Not at all. When he'd first believed that Emily was on the way to recovery, he'd envisioned the day when he could take her back to D.C., bid her a fond farewell, then fly down to Mississippi to take care of the matter that had been pressing on his heart and mind for months.

Angel.

His plan was to declare his love and try to win her back. If it wasn't too late.

That kind of thinking was dangerous. He refused to believe it was too late.

Instead, he hung his clothes in the closet at the Algonquin and told himself he could endure anything for a few more days.

Emily stuck her head around the door frame. "This bed is huge," she said.

"You can have the bed. I'll take the couch."

Was that a look of disappointment that crossed her face? Surely not.

Still, Emily was a strong-willed woman, accustomed to getting what she wanted.

Not for the first time, Steve questioned his judgment in going along with her plans. He needed air, he needed time alone, he needed to think.

"You finish unpacking, then rest and we'll go to the Tavern on the Green for dinner. I'm going to take a walk," he said, then headed to the door.

"Steve, wait. Can I come?"

She looked so vulnerable standing there with her slacks bagging and her hair hanging limp. His heart twisted. She *was* vulnerable. He knew from experience. He understood.

"Sure. I'm going to Central Park. Think you can make it that far?"

"You bet." The old Emily briefly flashed a smile, the trooper, the woman he'd married a long time ago. "If I see that I can't, I'll hail a cab back and you can go on without me. How's that?"

"Deal."

He shook her hand, and she held on. It was only natural, he told himself. Especially if you planned to stay together in the crowds that jostled and shoved along the sidewalks of New York.

She was panting and out of breath by the time they reached Central Park.

"Look, Steve. The horse-drawn carriages. Let's ride."

The ride through the park had always been a favorite of Emily's. He saw no harm in indulging her.

"Which one?" he said.

"You choose the horse. After all, you're the expert."

The only good thing about being in the buggy was that Emily was so tired she leaned back against the cushions and ceased her chatter. Since she'd given up the bottle, she'd taken up nonstop talking.

"Nice, huh?" She sighed and leaned her head against his shoulder.

He sat silently, enduring. In all their time at the ranch, Emily had never acted this way. Tomorrow he would definitely book himself into another hotel.

Or plead business and head back to Arizona. What difference would a few days possibly make to Emily? She was going to fly directly to D.C., anyhow.

The carriage drew to a halt as the crowd passed by—

shoppers laden with bags, bedraggled mothers hanging on to wide-eyed children, businessmen rushing to the next appointment, a beautiful blonde wearing a red wool cape.

Steve did a double take. Did he make a strangled sound, call out her name? She looked up, and he found himself staring into the incredible blue eyes of Angel Mercer.

''Steve.'' She said his name, soundless, her lips parted. Lush. Glossy. Delicious.

It was possible to drown in the eyes of another. Now Steve knew that. Simply drown for lack of oxygen.

Was his heart still beating, or was it possible for a heart to stand still, to wait for that next beat until Angel smiled, giving her blessing.

The crowd jostled her, but she was rooted to the spot, mesmerized as he. A gust of wind ruffled her hair and caught the hem of her cape, sending it swirling around her. It spooked the horse, and suddenly there was bedlam.

The driver pulled on the reins, yelling. Children scattered, screaming. Packages sailed through the air, landing willy-nilly on the street.

And Angel was in the midst of it all, the heavy carriage bearing down on her. Steve leaped from the buggy and swept her aside just as the carriage lurched by.

He cushioned her fall as they sprawled on the ground. He wrapped his arms tightly around her, loving the way she felt, welcoming her home, even with the taint of danger still in the air.

''Are you all right?''

Her face was so close he could see the gold starbursts in the center of her eyes. He could feel her warm breath fan his cheek. He could smell the fragrance of her skin.

He was in heaven.

He was in hell, because Angel was in his arms and Emily waited for him in the carriage.

"I'm fine."

She didn't pull away and hope leaped through him. The sun glinted in her shining hair, and he buried his face there. How could he resist?

"Angel," he murmured. "Angel." *I love you.*

The words were there in his heart, on the tip of his tongue, but this was neither the time nor the place to say them. There were a dozen things he had to know. How long was she staying in New York? Where was she staying? When could he see her?

A tremor ran through her, then she stiffened and pulled away. Steve helped her up, longing to pull her back into his arms.

"We need to talk, Angel."

Suddenly Emily bore down on them, thrusting a green-and-gold package toward Angel.

"You dropped this," she said, and the moment was shattered, like a pop bottle thrown on the sidewalk.

"Thanks," she said, her smile hesitant and a little strained.

Emily laced her arm through Steve's. "Can we go back to the hotel, Steve? I'm tired."

Angel whirled away from him and hurried off.

"Angel, wait," he called after her, but she never slowed her steps, never turned around.

"Can we take a cab, Steve?" Emily said.

He watched until Angel was out of sight.

"Yes," he said. "We can take a cab."

Angel stood in Jenny's sunny kitchen with her arms wrapped around herself.

"You're still shaking," Jenny said.

"I had a brush with danger."

"Yeah. Not from the horse, but from Thunderhorse."

Anger and love waged a war inside Angel, sometimes love winning out and sometimes anger. Impatiently she cast off her cape and stalked around the kitchen.

"Did I tell you that they were staying together in a hotel?"

"Twice."

"She had her head on his shoulder. On…his…shoulder."

Jenny was silent. She'd heard that, too. Probably more than once, but Angel didn't stop her tirade. That's what friends were for, to lend a shoulder to cry on.

"She looked better than she did in those interviews she gave the press last fall."

"That's too bad."

Angel felt like a witch, wishing Emily ill because she'd been sitting beside Steve with her head on his shoulder, because she was staying with him in a hotel, because she was with him. Period.

"He said we needed to talk. Why should I talk to him? He's left me twice."

"Remember that."

"Why should I care what he has to say?"

"Damned right."

Angel began to cry. The buzzer sounded, and Jenny told the doorman to send Britt up. He took one look, handed Angel his handkerchief and got out the coffeepot.

"I believe this is going to be a four-cup evening." He chucked Jenny under the chin. "What do you think, cupcake?"

Angel's tears had become full-fledged sobs.

"I think that for once I'm glad to see you."

The cab inched its way through the five-o'clock traffic. Steve endured. If he was alone, he'd be back at the hotel by now on the phone finding out where Angel was staying.

Emily sat on her side of the cab, her head leaned against the seat, strain showing in her face.

"Are you mad at me?" she said.

"Puzzled."

"Because I returned her package? Because I'm tired?"

Emily's voice had an edge. She was spoiling for a fight. He remembered well.

"The cab is not the place to talk," he said, but Emily was not deterred.

"All right. I admit it. I behaved like a possessive wife."

"Can we save this?"

"What? Till we get back to that suite where you've insisted on staking out the couch? I think not. Let's clear the air now."

"All right. Just don't mention names."

"Oh, the perfect Miss An—"

"Don't."

She turned her face to the window, and when she swiveled back she had tears in her eyes.

"I'm sorry," she said, and she seemed to mean it. "I don't know what I was thinking. Not really. It's just that you've been so good to me, and planning this trip brought back so many memories.... I guess I just thought we deserved one last chance. We were good together once. Remember?"

"Yes, but we were more a habit than a love match. Do you remember that? Our marriage was more a matter of convenience than of romance."

"You really love her, don't you?"

"Yes."

The Algonquin loomed ahead.

"I think I'd like to have dinner alone," she said. "Why don't you go inside and do what you have to do?" She caught his hand and squeezed hard. "She's getting a good man. Tell her that for me."

The yellow cab drove off with Emily, and Steve raced upstairs to the telephone.

Chapter Twenty-Six

By the time she'd had her second cup of coffee, Angel was coherent, and by the time she'd had her third, she was beginning to feel a giddy caffeine high.

"Enough," she said. "I won't sleep a wink."

"You won't sleep a wink, anyhow, after what happened today," Jenny said. "I know you. You'll want to be up the rest of the night talking." She poured herself another cup. "I don't know about you, but I like to be wide awake when I listen."

"Since when do you listen, Jenny?" Britt said. "You're too busy dispensing advice."

She threw a pillow at him. "If you're not careful I'm going to take you up on one of those bogus offers for dinner."

"They're not bogus. I'm a sensitive man and you've wounded me."

Their antics had Angel laughing, which was exactly what

they'd intended, and in the midst of it all Jenny's phone rang.

"Hello," Jenny said, then scowled. "She's not here."

Angel stiffened. "Thunderhorse?" she whispered.

"Yes," Jenny mouthed.

Angel grabbed the phone. "I'm here."

"Hello, Angel."

Steve's voice flowed through her veins like a wild river, and she was swept up in the current, caught off balance, tumbled about in the roaring waters until she was so weak she had to sit down.

"How did you find me?" she said.

"I called your dad."

"Dad told you?"

"Not until I convinced him of my true intentions."

She was shivering again. Jenny and Britt were watching her like mother hens over their only chick.

"I'm fine," Angel told them. "Go out and get a bagel."

"A bagel?" Steve said.

"Not you. Jenny and Britt."

"Are they there?"

"Not now. They just left."

"I'll be right over."

"No, Steve, wait," she said, but the line was already dead.

Steve was on his way here. To see her. To talk, he'd said.

Angel's mind whirled with possibilities. Should she dress for him? Definitely.

She raced into the guest bedroom, flinging off her clothes as she ran. What should she wear? Not white, not something filmy and old-fashioned. That was too obvious. She didn't want him to think she'd dressed to please him.

Or did she?

Angel sat on the edge of her bed. She didn't know what

she wanted. Her mind told her one thing and her heart another. She knew only that if Steve wanted her, this time it had to be for keeps. She could not endure another heartbreak.

Angel chose a black wool boot-length skirt and a blue cashmere sweater. She'd just finished running a brush through her hair when the buzzer sounded.

Steve was here.

Her sweater matched her eyes. That was the first thing Steve noticed. The next was how pale she was, as if she'd been crying.

"Hello, Angel," he said, so formally, as if they were strangers.

"Won't you come in?" she said, so politely, as if they had never lain tangled together in his big bed.

Now that he was here, he was as nervous as a teenager. He wanted to throw her over his shoulder and run as fast as he could all the way to Arizona, back to the ranch where he was master of his own fate, where he was at ease in his own skin, where the words in his heart would tumble freely from his lips.

There had been a time when he was as much at home in big cities as he was in wide-open spaces. But that was a lifetime ago. He was out of his element here, and he was glad.

Some people had told him he was throwing his talent away when he left photojournalism and moved out West. Some people said he was burying himself. What they didn't know was that he had actually freed himself. He'd chosen a simple life filled with simple pleasures. He'd chucked fame and fortune and found his soul.

And now he'd found love. But how to say it? How to make Angel believe it?

"Coffee?" she said.

"Yes."

Having a cup in his hand would give him something to do. When she gave him the cup, he caught her hand.

"Angel, I'm sorry if I've hurt you."

She pulled out of his grasp and sat as far away from him as possible. Clearly she was not going to make this easy for him.

"Well, you did, Steve. You hurt me terribly. Not once, but twice."

"That was never my intention. Please believe me."

She studied him a moment for answering.

"I believe you," she said. "But that doesn't change anything."

"Let me explain what you saw in the park," he said. "That was Emily."

"I recognized her…from her photograph in the newspapers."

"She was my wife, the mother of my child. I finally did what I should have done nine years ago. I brought her to the ranch so I could help her. Nothing more."

"How is she?"

"This time I think she's going to be all right. We talked. We've resolved a lot of issues that have been left hanging for too long."

Angel was silent, her hands folded in her lap, her eyes enormous and watchful.

"Emily is going back to D.C. after the parade," he added. "Alone."

He sounded like a newspaper reporter, even to himself. Nothing personal. No emotion. Just the facts. Angel was as remote as the summit of Mount Everest.

To hell with this, he thought. He was sitting on the sofa like some overcivilized fop while the woman he loved was not two feet away. Sitting Bull would be ashamed of him. His Sioux ancestors would disown him.

The blood of warriors boiled in his veins. The heart of the mighty plains Indians beat in his chest.

Thunderhorse rose from the couch, transformed. Angel's eyes widened, and she tried to scramble from her chair, but he caught her and pulled her into his arms.

"I've been wanting to kiss you ever since I walked into this room."

He took her lips fiercely, a hunter capturing his quarry, a warrior storming the fort, a Sioux brave staking his claim.

She put up a wildcat's fight, but her resistance melted quickly. Spreading his hands across the small of her back, he pulled her so close she lost her breath.

"I don't intend to let you go, Angel. Ever."

If he'd expected an easy victory, he was mistaken. Her color was high and her eyes were blazing. He was determined to win her, but she was equally determined to put up a fight.

"Let go of me," she said.

"Why? So you can sit stiffly in that chair, denying that you want me as much as I want you?"

He kissed her again, hard. So hard their chests were both heaving when they drew apart.

"Do you think I'm some...some Kewpie doll you can win at a county fair?"

"No, I think you're the most appealing flesh-and-blood woman I've met. And I want you more than I've ever wanted a woman in my life."

"Well, goody for you." She jerked out of his grasp and stalked to the window, where she turned her back to him.

If her stiff posture was any indication, her thoughts were as black as her mood.

He was doing this badly. What had he expected? He was

nine years out of practice. He had no more idea of how to win a woman than he had of how to scale the Empire State Building with his bare hands.

She whirled on him. "Do you think you can just waltz in here after all this time and start...start *mauling* me simply because that's what *you* want?"

"You've got this all wrong."

"Oh, *I'm* the one who has it all wrong? That's rich, Steve. You walk out on me in Arizona without so much as a fare-thee-well, you barely speak to me in Mississippi, and now you think I'm going to tumble back into your bed?"

"You have a stinger, Angel. I never knew that."

"There are lots of things you never knew, Steve. That I have a heart, for one thing. And that hearts are easily broken and not so easily mended."

"A big long stinger. I guess I'll just have to pull it out."

He pulled her against him, then tipped her face up with his forefinger.

"Did I tell you that I love you, Angel?"

"Why should I believe that? A man will say anything to get what he wants."

"Did I tell you that I want to spend the rest of my life with you?"

"Here? In Jenny's apartment? Down in Mississippi where it's so hot even your horse will sweat? Or would that be in Paradise?"

He chuckled. "All those places and more. Anywhere you like."

"Oh, I see. The man who won't even sit down beside me and give a simple statement at a press conference is suddenly willing to open his home to a woman who can't go twenty feet without an entourage? Or is that something you'd expect me to give up?"

"How much longer do you think you're going to be mad?"

"Why?"

"Because I'm dying to kiss you again."

And he did. Furthermore, she kissed him back. Her arms stole around his neck, her fingers wove into his hair, and she made the soft murmuring sounds of pleasure he loved.

He thought he'd won, then she proved him wrong.

"The answer is *no,* Steve. I won't go to Arizona and be told which horse to ride and when to ride and where. I won't run away and hide like some fugitive. I won't mold myself into something I'm not simply because that's the way you want it to be."

"Where does love fit into all this?"

"This is not about love, Steve. It's about power. I won't be controlled by somebody else. Never again."

She picked up the coffee cups and stomped into the kitchen. He hoped the china wasn't delicate.

He stood by the window, trying not to be anxious. Trying to tell himself that he couldn't lose, that victory was only minutes away. Maybe the Sitting Bull approach was all wrong. Maybe it didn't work without the horse.

He would give her time to cool off, then when she came back they would sit down and talk like civilized adults.

She was still steaming when she came back. He could tell by the way her eyes sparked fire.

Steve watched her with admiration. This was a side of Angel he'd never seen, a spunky fiery determination she would pass on to her children.

Children?

Where had that thought come from? He'd never thought about children, not after Sunny, and yet here he was, not only trying to win the woman he loved, but planning a full-blown future with her, one that included children and all the risks involved.

He waited for that quiet shrinking within himself, that rebellion against being responsible for a small helpless human being, one he might not always be able to protect. Nothing happened but the assurance that he loved and loved deeply, and that love was worth any risk.

"I don't want to control you, Angel. I merely want to love you, to have a home with you, to have children with you."

"Children?"

"You don't want children?"

"Yes, but..." She jumped out of her chair as if she'd been shot. "The subject is moot. I don't even want to go to Arizona with you, let alone have children with you."

The rosy blush on her face belied her words.

"Why would I want to have children with a man who just pulls up stakes and runs whenever he takes a notion, without so much as a word to the woman he professes to love?"

"I told you what that was all about, Angel. There were some things I had to straighten out first."

"Couldn't you have said that to me beforehand? Couldn't you have said, 'Angel, there are some things I need to take care of—I'll be back'?"

"I didn't think it fair to ask you to wait."

"See? You make all the decisions, Steve. Why didn't you ask me if I thought it was fair? Why didn't you let me in on a few of the plans?"

"Habit. Pride. Fear." He knelt beside her and took her hand. "Angel, I love you. Whatever problems we have, we can work out. Together."

Eyes misted over, she brushed his hair back from his forehead.

"I wish I had Muriel's gifts," she whispered. "I wish I could see the future."

"You don't need Muriel's gifts. I'll show you the future."

Releasing her, he pulled the frayed pink ribbon out of his pocket. Angel made a soft sound of surprise.

"I've carried your ribbon over my heart since the day I left you in Mississippi. Sometimes at night when I couldn't sleep for thinking of you, I would take the ribbon to bed so I could have a small part of you beside me."

He turned her hands over and placed a tender kiss in each palm.

"Marry me, Angel."

"I think I'm going to cry."

"You already are."

He brushed her tears away with his thumbs.

"I don't know what to say," she whispered.

"You don't have to say anything. Not right now." Leaning over her, Steve tied the pink ribbon around her neck. "I want you to come to me freely, without pressure and without reservations."

"Steve—"

"Shh." He traced her lips with his fingers. "When you're ready, you'll let me know your answer. Until then, I'll be waiting."

Bending over, he tucked a slip of paper with the hotel's number in her hand, then kissed her softly. Leaving her again was one of the hardest things he'd ever had to do. He did it quickly before he could change his mind.

Chapter Twenty-Seven

Steve wore a path in the rug at the Algonquin waiting for Angel to call. He missed the parade, which he hadn't really wanted to see in the first place. He took meals in his room.

Emily stuck her head around the doorway. "What time does your plane leave?"

"I don't know." How could he leave New York when Angel was here?

"You don't have to snarl."

"Sorry. I have things on my mind.... What are you laughing at?"

"You. Giving up control has turned you into a grizzly bear."

Was he that bad? Steve wondered. Probably. He had never willingly relinquished control. Everything in his being wanted to storm Jenny's apartment, throw Angel over his shoulder and head to the nearest justice of the peace.

But if he did that he would never know whether he had

won her heart or merely won a victory. There was only one thing for Steve to do: Get on the plane and go home to wait.

"Are you all set?" he asked Emily.

"Ready. Bags packed and waiting."

"I'll call a cab."

"Steve, wait. Before you do I want to say one thing. I sincerely wish nothing but the best for you."

"Same here." He hugged her close, feeling how thin she was, how fragile. "Stay well, Emily. And if you need me for anything, anything at all, call me. Day or night. I'll be there for you."

"I know you will. But guess what, Steve? I can make it now on my own. Women can, you know. Try to remember that."

He gave her a rueful grin. "I'll try."

The frayed pink ribbon was a constant reminder to Angel of all that Steve had said, all that he'd promised, but it was her dad's wedding that did her in.

He promised to love, honor and cherish Kaki for the rest of his days, forsaking all others, and Angel knew that at last she was truly alone. She could do exactly as she pleased. All the time. Nobody to tell her what to do. Not that Carl ever had. Still, she would be all by herself in that big house, keeping her own schedule, marching to her own drummer.

Something twisted inside her. The plain fact was this: There was only one tune she wanted to march to, and that was the tune of love.

But how was she going to tell Thunderhorse? A phone call was much too mundane. A love as stormy, passionate and magnificent as theirs deserved a grand gesture.

"Angel...Angel." Jenny was talking to her.

"What?"

"Come on, Kaki's getting ready to throw the bouquet."

"*You're* going to try to catch the bouquet?"

"You never know." Jenny blushed, a first for her.

"Will wonders never cease."

The words were no sooner out of Angel's mouth than the wedding bouquet sailed her way and landed smack-dab in the middle of her arms.

"And I wasn't even trying," she said. But of course, she had been, unconsciously, for every Southern woman worth her salt knew that catching a bouquet was a sign of good luck. For what she was going to do, Angel was going to need it, and plenty of it.

Kaki and Carl came up to hug her and to tell her goodbye. For their honeymoon, they were spending two months in Europe.

"Goodbye, sweetheart," Carl said. "Take good care of yourself. We'll call. We'll write."

"You do no such thing. You go off and have fun."

"I plan to see that he does," Kaki said, laughing.

Britt drove the honeymooners to the airport, and Angel went home to discuss her plans with Jenny. After she had finished talking, Jenny wiped her eyes and blew her nose.

"I didn't know you'd take the news so hard, Jenny."

"I'm not taking the news hard. Happy endings always make me cry."

"You think this will be a happy ending, then?"

Jenny smiled. "Yes, I do, Angel. For all of us."

Lucas was off on his motorcycle, God only knew where, and Wayne had gone off and bought the biggest tree he could find, then came dragging it back to the house, grinning like an idiot.

"What am I supposed to do with that thing?"

Steve figured he sounded worse than a sore-tailed cat, but he didn't care. That was exactly how he felt.

Three weeks and not a single word from Angel. It was enough to drive him insane.

"It's a Christmas tree. For Christmas, remember? Deck the halls, Rudolph the Red-Nosed Reindeer, ho-ho-ho and all that jazz."

Wayne looked aggrieved. And long-suffering. Since Lucas had been gone, Wayne had borne the entire brunt of Steve's discontent.

"Ho-ho-ho," Steve said.

"Where do you want me to put it?"

"How about out in the barn?"

"Very funny."

Wayne dragged the damned thing into the hallway while Steve flipped on the television to watch the news. Maybe world events would take his mind off Angel.

"Anything else you need before I go, Steve?"

"No thanks."

Wayne looked anxious standing in the doorway. And worried.

Steve felt like Ebenezer Scrooge.

"Thanks for the tree, Wayne. Tell Martha and the children Merry Christmas for me."

"You bet. Hope it's a good one for you, too, Steve."

How could it possibly be good with Angel in Mississippi and him in Arizona? If he didn't hear something from her soon, he was going to...

"Do nothing," he said, disgusted with himself. "I'm going to do absolutely nothing but wait."

Angel either wanted him or she didn't. She either loved him or she didn't.

The news was winding down, and he hadn't heard a word they'd said. He started to flip the television off when an announcement caught his eye. "Special Feature," it read. "Christmas with Angel Mercer."

His heart did a flip-flop. When? The bulletin had flashed off now, and a silly game show was on. Steve snatched up the TV guide and began a frantic search. There it was. Eight o'clock.

He just had time for dinner before her show. Leaving the TV blaring so he could hear it in the kitchen, he raced to the refrigerator and dished up a bowl of leftover stew.

What if he'd read wrong? What if that was eight o'clock eastern time? Or central time?

Grabbing a spoon, he hurried back to the den and sat down in front of the TV with his cold stew. An eternity later, there she was, Angel, filling the screen, her smile beautiful and somewhat wistful.

She was wearing pink, something old-fashioned and graceful-looking that floated around her legs when she walked. The camera followed her as she moved through her house—there, the hallway where he'd stood with her in his arms, and there, the winding staircase where he carried her upstairs. The camera veered to the living room where an enormous tree stood in the corner. Angel sat in a wing chair beside the tree and talked about the Christmases she'd known in Mississippi.

"Every year Mother and Daddy and I made ornaments," she said. "When I was six I made this dough angel."

The camera panned in close to show a crooked angel, purple with pink wings and sporting a red halo.

"Even then you were showing your creative talents."

Britt Ace was the interviewer. Who else? He was good, though. Smooth. And he seemed to have a special rapport with Angel.

Steve leaned forward, hanging on every word.

"You had a wonderful childhood, didn't you?" Britt was saying. "Happy, well adjusted, filled with love."

"Yes." Angel smiled. "I want to pass that on to my children."

Her children? Steve turned up the volume.

"Remember, folks, you heard that on ABS." Britt smiled for the camera. "Earlier this evening Miss Mercer indicated that she had news regarding her career that she would reveal to us on this broadcast. Angel, what is that news?"

"I'm taking an extended sabbatical from writing."

Steve was out of his seat, squatting three inches in front of his television, drinking in Angel's every word.

"Does this mean there won't be any more stories about your popular gumshoe angel, Muriel?"

"At this time, no, I don't plan a sequel."

"Are you saying there is a possibility for one sometime in the future?"

"Anything is possible. Anything at all."

"Does your decision to take a break from writing have anything to do with a man named Thunderhorse?"

Steve forgot to breathe.

"Love is not for public record."

Angel smiled as the camera panned in close, and there around her neck was the tattered pink ribbon.

Chapter Twenty-Eight

It had been three days since the broadcast and Steve still hadn't called. Angel stood in front of her tree, staring at the lights as if they were crystal balls and she could see the future.

What if he hadn't seen the broadcast? What if he had seen it and no longer cared?

This kind of thinking could drive her crazy. Tomorrow she would call him. Period. She would communicate the good old-fashioned way. By telephone.

"Steve," she would say. "My answer is yes. If you still want me, I'll marry you."

What if he wasn't home? What if he said no?

Angel paced, she worried, she fretted. A streak of gold coming through the window nearly blinded her. She went to the window to adjust the shades against the setting sun, and that was when she saw the brass band lining up on her lawn.

Now what? A bizarre fan club sending her Christmas greetings? A prank? A kook?

They were tuning up now, and if the squawking and honking were any indications, she was in for a rude awakening.

Furthermore, they were probably trampling her flower beds.

"I'll call the police."

She was reaching for the phone when the band started playing. The music was beautiful, haunting, familiar.

Suddenly Angel was running toward the door, arms wide open. The song they were playing was "Embraceable You."

And there was Steve Thunderhorse in buckskins and beaded moccasins, thundering her way on his white stallion.

She shaded her eyes against the red-gold sun. When he drew even with her, he halted.

"Did you save the last dance for me, Angel?"

"Yes," she said.

He swung her onto the white stallion, and while the band played their song, they danced.

"You dance well as long as you have the horse," she said, teasing him.

"I do many things well."

"With the horse?"

"Without. Would like me to show you?"

"Here? Now?"

"There's another place I have in mind. A place called Paradise. Would you care to go there with me?"

"Yes. Now and forever."

And as the last strains of their song faded away, Angel rode off into the sunset with the man she loved.

She couldn't have written the ending better herself.

* * * * *

*Let Peggy Webb sweep you off your feet
with her next passionate romance,*

GRAY WOLF'S WOMAN,

*available September 2000
in Special Edition,
only from Silhouette Books.*

Here's a sneak peak!

Lucas came upon the woman suddenly, just as he topped the ridge near the cave where he'd found Rusty. She looked as if she'd come from combat in a small and dusty country. Her red hair was disheveled, her cheeks were smudged, and her shirttail was untucked. She had a miniature replica of herself perched on one hip and another angelic child by the hand.

When she saw them, she picked up the biggest stick she could find, then took up a wide-legged stance in front of her little girls, a she-bear getting ready to fight for her young.

It looked as if Lucas had found Rusty's mother. He brought his bike to a halt.

"If you come near me or my girls I'll make you sorry you were ever born," she said.

Lucas smiled. "Rusty's already done that. This morning."

She raised the stick, and Lucas suppressed a laugh. She

was so tiny he could easily tuck her under his arm and carry her off if he wanted to. Which he absolutely did not. No matter how appealing that gleaming cap of red-gold curls was. What in the world would he do with a woman with three children?

Protect her.

The minute the thought whispered through his mind, Lucas knew he was in trouble. If anybody needed protection, it was Rusty's mom. The little redhead sitting on the ground behind her was sucking her thumb, clinging to her baby doll and crying, and the little blonde squatting beside her sister looked as if she didn't know whether to fight or cry.

And Lucas already knew enough about the hellion on his motorbike to feel enormous sympathy for the woman facing him with a stick half as big as she was.

"My name is Lucas Gray Wolf. I rescued your son from the bottom of a cave."

She wavered between disbelief and gratitude. "That's a likely story."

"I didn't kidnap your child, lady. As a matter of fact, I'll pay you to take him back."

"How much you gonna give for me, Gray Wolf?"

"Rusty Belinda, you tell me the truth this minute, or when I get you back home you'll be the sorriest little boy on the block. Did this man kidnap you?"

"Naw. I run off 'cause I was sick of girls. Then I was gonna explore this ol' cave, see? Gray Wolf got me out, but I could'a got out myself."

"I'm afraid I've been very rude to you, Mr. Gray Wolf."

"Call me Lucas. Please."

"And I'm Mandy, Mandy Belinda."

Her name dripped off her tongue like warm honey, and he wanted to hear her say it again, but he dared not ask. He dared not do anything except stand still and try to learn how to breathe again.

"I have some homemade brownies back at the camp. Do say you'll come and share a brownie with us. It's the least I can do."

If she'd offered him a meal, he might have declined. If she'd offered him a cool drink, even as hot as it was, he might have had the sense to say no. But she was offering him the one thing he couldn't resist—chocolate.

"I'd like that," he said, knowing all the time that he should get on his bike and ride the other way as fast as he could, knowing that if she smiled at him in that sparkly way again he was going to be in big trouble.

That's how he ended up at her campsite sitting at a picnic table provided by the park, eating the best brownies he'd ever put in his mouth, and watching Mandy with more than passing interest.

ENTER FOR A CHANCE TO WIN*

Silhouette's 20th Anniversary Contest

Tell Us Where in the World You Would Like *Your* Love To Come Alive... And We'll Send the Lucky Winner There!

Silhouette wants to take you wherever your happy ending can come true.

Here's how to enter: Tell us, in 100 words or less, where you want to go to make your love come alive!

In addition to the grand prize, there will be 200 runner-up prizes, collector's-edition book sets autographed by one of the Silhouette anniversary authors: **Nora Roberts, Diana Palmer, Linda Howard** or **Annette Broadrick**.

DON'T MISS YOUR CHANCE TO WIN! ENTER NOW! No Purchase Necessary

Silhouette®
Where love comes alive™

Visit Silhouette at www.eHarlequin.com to enter, starting this summer.

Name: _____

Address: _____

City: _____ State/Province: _____

Zip/Postal Code: _____

Mail to Harlequin Books: **In the U.S.**: P.O. Box 9069, Buffalo, NY 14269-9069; **In Canada**: P.O. Box 637, Fort Erie, Ontario, L4A 5X3